THE HAPPIEST PLACE

ALASKAN HEARTS, BOOK 6

MELISSA STORM

Editor: Megan Harris
Cover by Daqri Bernardo at Covers by Combs

Partridge & Pear Press
PO Box 72
Brighton, MI 48116

To all who cherish the irreplaceable memories of childhood

ABOUT THIS BOOK

Kate can't believe she's losing her mother. For as long as she can remember, it's been the two of them against the world. That is, until early-onset Alzheimer's robbed them both of the relationship that had always been so special.

Kate accepted a job at Memory Ranch to keep an eye on her mom, but is left wonder whether she's the one who really needs to heal. Especially as a certain handsome therapist named Jack keeps finding more and more reasons for them to spend time together.

What will be left of Kate when her mother leaves her behind? And can she justify spending time with Jack when she knows her mom's time left on earth is limited?

CHAPTER 1

KATE GRIFFIN LEANED HER HEAD AGAINST THE COOL GLASS window and watched the horses in the pen as they frolicked in the fresh snowfall. They playfully kicked the white powder over their backs and tossed their manes in delight as it sprinkled down onto their necks. Even from where she was sitting, Kate could practically feel the pure joy emanating from the animals.

Smiling to herself, she wrapped her arms around her shivering body, all the while wishing she could be out there with them. Unfortunately, her work in the stables had been cut short for the day when her mother's health took another sudden turn for the worse.

Kate lifted her head from the glass and glanced toward the back of the cabin where she could see her mother sleeping on the bed. She'd left the door to the small bedroom open so she could keep an eye on her mom just in case.

For the past few months, they'd been living together in one of the guest cabins at Memory Ranch, a memory care and therapy center outside of Anchorage. Here, Kate worked as a stable hand, and her mother underwent treatment for early onset Alzheimer's disease. Initially, Kate had obtained the job as a way of checking out the facilities firsthand to see if they'd be a good fit for her mother's increasingly heavy needs. It didn't take long to realize it was exactly what they both needed.

The disease had snuck up on both of them. One day her mother was fine, and the next she was forgetting increasingly big details of their lives. Kate didn't have time to adapt to the news, and her mom didn't have the capacity to fully understand it. Always a sharp-witted woman, the sudden memory decline frustrated her to tears most days. For her part, Kate prayed that the day would come soon when her mother didn't remember enough to know she was forgetting.

Of course, that would mean she'd lost the last remnants of herself, too, but at least she wouldn't be afraid or in pain any longer.

Now that they had settled into the life at the ranch, Kate saw how her mother was receiving the care she needed from the special therapists who were trained to work with people who suffered from memory trauma. And hopefully they could help her, too, as she came to terms with what was happening with her mom.

Turning back to watch the horses playing in the snow, Kate sighed, her breath fogging the window. She let her mind wander back to before everything in her world had fallen apart. Before they'd ever heard the diagnosis.

All her life, it had just been Kate and her mom. Her father had run out when she was just a baby and hadn't been seen since. Truthfully, Kate didn't even care. Anyone who could abandon their family wasn't anyone she wanted to know.

Her mom stepped up to play the role of both parents and had done a phenomenal job. They'd never had much, but her mom had worked hard to make sure they had enough to get by. For many years, her mother had worked as part of the cleaning staff at a ranch in Palmer, Alaska, and Kate had spent many of her earliest days watching the horses and wishing she might someday have one of her own.

Of course, they'd never had enough money to buy one for her—or the space to put one up in their modest apartment. Still, Kate had been content to claim the horses on the ranch as her pets, her friends, and her confidantes.

To this day, she still dreamed of having a horse to call her own, but for now she counted working at this ranch, where she could be around horses all day and still be able to care for her mom, as a massive blessing.

Kate felt blessed for the opportunity, but her heart still cried out in pain at the unfairness of what her mother's life had become. After everything her mom had been through—being left to care for and raise a child on her own, struggling to make ends meet and never taking time for herself—now the very essence of who she was slowly being stolen from her.

And her disease was moving fast, leaving a shell in place of the woman who'd given Kate her everything—the strong, beautiful woman who had always been her best friend, her cheerleader, and her rock.

The doctors had road-mapped how the disease was most likely to progress and the corresponding issues they would face at each stage. However, none of it had prepared Kate for the emotional strain that came with watching her mother forget even the simplest of things or witness her personality changing practically overnight.

At least through it all, so far, she still remembered Kate.

That awful day would come, though. And soon.

Kate's stomach churned in agony from the mere thought of becoming a stranger to the person she loved most in this entire world. She would never be ready.

How was she going to live without the one person who loved her beyond reason and who she loved in turn with her whole heart, too? How could she go on with life when so many of her formative memories—the moments that made her *her*—were rapidly being erased from memory?

Kate reached up to wipe away the tear that slid down her cheek. So many tears had been shed, but the well hadn't yet dried up.

In the pen, Buddy, the beautiful, kind-hearted tan horse, stopped running and looked over toward the cabin window where she sat, seeming to feel her emotions himself. How she wished she could go hop on his back and ride away from everything that was happening in her life.

But her mom needed her, and this was where she had to be. She would give all of herself until there was nothing left to give, and no one left to give it to.

"Kate? Are you there?" came her mother's small and scared voice.

Kate quickly turned and walked to the room. "I'm here, Mom. I was just watching the horses playing outside. Did you have a good rest?" she asked as she knelt down at her mom's bedside.

Her mom sat up, pushing the warm quilt away. Her quiet smile was filled with warmth, and her eyes sparkled with an untold joy. Briefly, Kate wondered how long until that was gone, too.

She nodded. "I did."

They each sighed and then laughed at this unexpected

synchronicity. It had been a joke they'd shared growing up, that their minds were telepathically linked—so similar they were then. Did this mean it was only a matter of time before Kate's memories began to fade, too?

Her mother was the first to sober from this rare bout of laughter. She frowned as she traced the wrinkles in her night dress with a shaky finger. "I'm sorry for yelling at you earlier. It wasn't fair. I know you're only doing what's best for me. It's just hard for me to accept sometimes."

When Kate had been called away from work earlier, it had been to collect her mother who'd wandered outside and was yelling at one of the other guests, wanting to know what he was doing in "her" yard. Mother and daughter had fought as Kate brought her back into their cabin and struggled to explain their situation yet again.

Although Kate had remained calm and kind, her mother's barbs stung deep. She tried to remind herself that the cruel accusations weren't coming from her mom, but from the disease that had taken over her mom's body.

Now that they were both more rested, everything seemed to revert to their old normal. But Kate knew it wouldn't last long. Already the time between bad spells had shrunk at a shocking pace. Eventually the lucid periods would disappear altogether.

Kate sat down beside her mom on the bed and reached a hand toward hers. Her mother, who had always seemed so big and strong, was now sitting there looking incredibly frail —as if her memories weren't the only part of her fading into oblivion.

Even with her reduced capacity, she still loved Kate as best she could. And she tried so hard to protect her from what was coming and what had already arrived.

Even in her worst, she wanted Kate to be taken care of.

"It's okay, Mom. Don't worry about it. All I want is for you to know how much I love you," she said, squeezing her mother's hand and offering a beleaguered smile. "If there's something you should never ever forget, it's that." The words threatened to crack as they left Kate's lips. There would come a time when even this indisputable fact would no longer be remembered.

Kate sat there for a long time, holding her mom tightly as each woman did her best to not let the other know she was crying, both wishing they could keep holding on to each other forever. Of course, Kate knew that someday she would have to let go. But for now, she was going to enjoy every precious moment she could wrapped tight in her mother's arms.

CHAPTER 2

KATE WOKE UP THE NEXT DAY SURROUNDED BY DARKNESS. Of course, winter in Alaska meant you were normally waking up in darkness and then going to bed in darkness, too. This had never really bothered her before, but these days she viewed everything through the lens of her mother's illness. How would she handle the dark in the winter? Or for that matter, the sun all summer?

She dressed quickly, mentally bracing herself for the possibility that her mother would wake up confused again. Instead, she opened her mom's door to find her dressed and reading a thick paperback book.

"Good morning, sleepyhead," her mom called out. "Are you ready to head up to the big house?" The main ranch estate where the owners, Elizabeth Jane and Dorian lived, also hosted their meals and other shared events in their day-to-day lives.

"Sure am. Are you ready for me to come to therapy with you?" Kate asked as she grabbed their coats from the hooks by the front door.

Her mother stepped out into the cold morning air before accepting her jacket and shivered. "No, I think you should just head to the stables."

"Are you sure you don't want me to stay with you this time?" Kate asked, pulling her gloves on as she walked beside her mom along the path to the main house. Besides the big dining area, the beautiful, old farmhouse had also been lovingly converted into multiple therapy rooms and rehabilitation stations.

The therapist who oversaw Kate's mom's care came out from his practice in Anchorage three times a week to hold sessions for the guests. He was a specialist for patients with memory disorders and had been working with her mother for several weeks. Kate didn't know much about what took place during the sessions—only that they differed from the occupational therapy her mother had no qualms about inviting her to attend.

"Not this time," her mom said, tucking her hands into her pockets after finally shrugging on her coat. "But Doctor Jack says I'm going to have to let you start coming to our sessions soon." She sighed heavily. "I know there are things you need to deal with, too, but right now I still feel like I need to be on my own. I hope you can understand."

Kate looped her arm through her mother's as they continued their journey toward the big house. The last part of the season was always the worst of the winter, making the short walk a hazardous one. Soon breakup would be upon them, heralding the beginning of spring, but today the air hung cold and thick around them. At least the day's forecast called for sunshine, which meant they might get a little extra warmth when it finally shone down on the cold ground below.

When they'd crossed the most slippery part of the path, Kate said, "I understand, Mom, don't worry. As long as therapy is helping you, don't worry about me. Right now, you're the one who needs to be cared for."

"That's not true, and you know it. You need to be cared for just as much as I do." Her mother's voice shook as she scolded her daughter. "I can see how much this is wearing you down, too. Please promise me you will take care of you first and foremost. I know the day will come that I won't be myself anymore and I won't be able to tell you to do things as a mother, so I need you to remember me saying it to you now. Don't forget to look after yourself. *You* are the priority."

Kate swallowed the lump in her throat and gave her mom a brave smile. "I will. I promise." She hoped the words would convince her mom, even though she wasn't sure she agreed with them. How could she worry about herself when it was her mom who was losing everything?

They walked up the front steps onto the large veranda and quickly opened the door to get in from the wet cold outside. A long coat rack hung beside the entryway, and Kate helped her mother out of the jacket she'd only just put on a few minutes prior. As she was struggling with the zipper on her own coat, her mother's therapist, Jack Young, appeared from the back with a warm smile stretched across his face.

Kate had seen him around the ranch quite a few times since she'd begun working here, and he had always extended a smile and a friendly greeting. Every time she saw him, her heart did a little somersault. It frustrated her to know she might have a school-girl crush on her mother's therapist, especially since this wasn't really the time to be getting all lovey-eyes with anyone. She needed to focus on her mom and on spending as much time with her as possible.

The last thing she needed was a man intruding on whatever little time they had left.

"Hi, Nancy! Kate." He nodded a greeting to her, and she found herself holding her breath when he looked directly into her eyes. The smile on his face caused his eyes to crinkle around the edges, and a slight dimple peeked out under the shadow of his whiskers. As long as she'd known him, she'd never seen Jack completely clean-shaven. He always had just a hint of a neatly trimmed five o'clock shadow dusting his chin and cheeks.

His dark hair was neatly swept back, except for a small curl that seemed to fall forward on its own accord. Kate found it completely adorable and immediately her cheeks started to burn as she realized she was now staring at that errant curl with a dreamy smile on her face as he continued to speak to her mom.

He probably thought she was the one who should be coming to therapy the way she was standing there staring at him like some kind of uncultured nitwit.

"Are you staying today?" he asked her with what almost looked like a hopeful glance. "I've told your mom that she's going to need you to start coming to at least some of her sessions, too, since you're her caregiver. Not to mention you're her daughter and I know the situation has to be difficult for you to navigate through, too."

Kate's heart skipped a beat as his deep voice rumbled in her ear.

Knock it off, Kate! He's a professional therapist working with your mother and that's what you should be focusing on right now!

She swallowed hard, groping for an answer. "No...um, no. Mom said she'd like another session alone. But maybe next time."

Why is my voice trembling? She hoped he couldn't discern her relief at being able to avoid him for at least one more day. Even though she knew she had to take part in a joint session—and wanted to on her mother's account—she didn't look forward to spending so much time discussing the most intimate details of her life with Jack.

Sometimes she felt it was just easier to pretend nothing had changed, that one day her mother would wake up and be back to her normal, zany self. Even as she watched her mom's health decline daily, she still held onto that sliver of impossible hope. Hearing the cold, hard truth from a man she felt inexplicably enamored of would be a double slap to the face.

She wasn't ready for that.

Besides, stalling her attendance at therapy for one more day wasn't going to hurt anyone.

"That's fine. As long as you're not just trying to avoid me." He chuckled, giving her a playful pat on the shoulder.

Kate's stomach knotted and for a moment she wondered if she was going to be sick, but then Jack put his professional face back on and the butterflies winging around in her stomach finally took a rest.

"I'll walk your mom back to your cabin when we're finished so you can go back to work, or whatever you were doing," he said, his fleeting grin lighting up the room once more.

Her mother chose that exact moment to join their conversation, and Kate was grateful for it. "I don't need you to walk me anywhere, young man. I'm still perfectly capable of getting around on my own. It's not like I have to ford rivers or climb mountains. It's just a little path."

Kate glanced toward Jack who was still smiling at her mom, but his expression seemed a bit sadder now.

"You're right, Nancy. But you also need to realize that there will be a time when you might not remember exactly where you need to go. It's too cold outside today for me to risk having today be that day. It would make me feel better if I knew I could get you safely home." He looked at Kate. "And I know it would make your daughter feel better, too."

She nodded in agreement, causing her mom to throw her hands up in frustration.

"Fine. It's not like I have any say anymore in what happens to me," she spat.

Kate cringed at the show of her mother's ugly temper coming out so early in the day. This did not bode well for them, but she waited to see how Jack would handle it.

He simply reached out for her mom's hand and placed it on his arm so he could lead her into his office in the back. As they walked away from her, Kate overheard him say, "Thank you, Nancy. And I know it feels like everything is being taken from you, but you still have control over many things, including how you deal with what's happening to you. And from what I've witnessed so far, you've been one of the strongest women I've ever met."

Immediately, her mom's anger drained from her face and she smiled sheepishly up at him. "I'm not strong. I'm just doing the best I can to be able to stay with my daughter as long as I can."

It seemed Kate wasn't the only Griffin woman to be befuddled by his charms. She watched them until the door swung shut behind them. Jack was right about one thing, and that was how strong her mother was now, had always been.

Now she just needed to find her own strength so she could make it through this, too.

CHAPTER 3

THE MAIN THING MEMORY RANCH WAS KNOWN FOR WAS its award-winning equestrian therapy program, and Kate was beyond honored to contribute in her small way, even if it was often just mucking out the stables or giving the horses a bit of exercise. She never would have dreamed she could find work doing what she loved while supporting the person she loved most in this world, too. She found her work with the horses centering in a world that often spun too fast for her to keep up.

Kate grabbed some hay and shook it through the fence into the feeding trough. She laughed as Buddy, the big tan horse, raced over as though he hadn't eaten for days. The horses were all brought up to live in the stables and pens in the small pasture during the winter. In fact, their state-of-the-art stables were bigger than one of the earlier apartments Kate and her mom had lived in after her father left.

"Buddy, just wait," she said, grabbing another section of the bale to shake out. "You've got to let me spread some of it out in the feeder so some of the others can eat, too."

She shook her head as she put the hay in the feeder, and the tan gelding followed her with his giant, groping lips. Working outside with the horses provided more healing than she'd ever manage to find stuck between four walls. As long as she could keep herself busy, she didn't have to think about the future or what might happen next.

For their part, the horses made for the most wonderful distractions, keeping her feet firmly planted in the present moment.

She shuffled the hay around, moving it so the other horses could reach the food, too. Buddy nudged her arm, trying to sneak some more hay. Laughing, she grabbed a little more hay to toss to Buddy.

As she stood back up to toss the hay in, her eyes landed on a figure in a heavy coat walking along the path toward her. Doctor Jack smiled as he approached. White breathy vapors escaped from his mouth as he adjusted his black wool cap to cover his ears.

"I didn't realize it was this cold outside today," he called out as he got closer. "It felt a lot warmer when I arrived earlier, but I guess going from my car into the house doesn't give me much chance to see how cold it really is." He brought his hands up to cup them in front of his mouth and blow in them. He smiled kindly at her again as she took a deep breath to calm her racing heart.

"You should be wearing gloves. We haven't even gotten to breakup season yet. It's going to be cold." She turned slightly to throw the next bit of hay over the fence, hoping he didn't catch her rolling her eyes at herself. She sounded like her mother had when she used to remind Kate about how she shouldn't be outside without her mittens.

Why was she even chiding him? It wasn't like her silly crush would ever amount to anything more. A doctor like Jack Young probably had women throwing themselves at his feet, flirting and acting coy whenever he was around. Kate knew the type. Jack was a good-looking and educated man who probably viewed her as some kind of small-town country hick who didn't know how to act around proper company.

Why was she thinking about all of this anyway? He worked as her mother's therapist, for crying out loud! He was trying to help them deal with just about the worst possible thing a family could go through, and here she was thinking how much he made her pulse quicken whenever he stood near to her.

He made a dismissive gesture, laughing at himself. "Oh, I know. I grew up not too far from here, so you'd think I would know better. But by the end of winter I'm just so ready for spring to be here, I forget it actually isn't."

Jack stepped closer to her and shoved his hands into his pockets. "I just dropped Nancy off at your cabin, so I thought you'd like to know. She was pretty tired by the end of the session, so I imagine she'll sleep for a while, but you might want to check in on her soon."

She flung the last bit of hay to the other side then leaned against the fence, unable to look him in the eyes as she spoke. "I figure you can't really discuss much about your sessions with her, but how do you feel about how things are progressing? I'm worried because it just seems like everything's happening so fast. She's having more and more bad spells lately. I honestly don't even like leaving her alone in the cabin for longer than a few minutes."

He nodded slowly and glanced over toward the row of cabins that could be seen just beyond the trees. "It's hard to say. Everyone is different, but she's showing all of the classic signs that the illness is continuing to progress quickly. I wish I could give you a timeline of some sort, but there really are no guarantees. Most patients only have four to eight years from the time of their diagnosis, but some keep going as long as twenty. As long as she's able to function well enough at home with you, I don't think there's any concern."

He turned back to face her and held her gaze with his deep brown eyes. "Have you been looking into options for more permanent full-time care for her when it gets to that point? I can help you find a suitable placement for her. I've worked with most facilities in Anchorage so I know which ones can offer the best care."

She shook her head firmly and turned to walk back toward the barn. She'd had this conversation many times before—with Jack, with the doctors, even with her own mother. "No. I can look after her. I'm not putting her in a home with people who don't even know her. She deserves better than that."

Jack caught up to her and placed a hand on her shoulder to stop her. Desperately trying to hold back tears, Kate refused to turn around and look at him.

"I know you want to look after Nancy yourself, but things are going to get harder. As good as your intentions are, you aren't equipped for the type of round-the-clock care she's going to need. Eventually she will get to the point of needing everything done for her. As much as you love her, that's not what she wants for you. And it's not something you can handle on your own."

She knew every word he said was true, but she wasn't ready to face this particular reality right now. "Mom raised me on her own and did everything all by herself, too. She's seen me through the roughest points in my life. The least I can do is treat her with the same level of care. If that means finding someone to come in and help, then that's what I'll do. But I'm not putting her in some home. I'm going to be there for her like she was for me." She still refused to look him in the eye.

Jack moved around to the front of her, forcing her to face him. Her eyes were wet from the tears she'd been holding back all morning. She kept them unfocused now, staring off toward the barn doors in the distance.

"Listen, it's a noble goal, and I know how hard it is. I really do. But I think you should talk to Nancy about this. She's told me many times that she doesn't want to be a burden on you."

He put his hands up to stop her when she glared at him, ready to tell him her mother would never be a burden. "Her words, not mine," he insisted. "I know you would never think like that, but you need to understand how your mother feels about all this. Please, come to the next session with her so we can sit down and give your mother the chance to talk to you about everything that's worrying her."

Kate narrowed her gaze in annoyance. "Do you think we haven't talked about all of this since she was diagnosed? Do you honestly believe I've just lived in a little bubble trying to ignore this disease? Do you think I don't already know everything she's feeling? Trust me, we've been over it all a hundred times since the diagnosis. I know where things are headed. And I'm going to do what's best for my mom. Right now, I think—no, I know—that's for her to be with me."

Just because Jack was a well-educated therapist didn't mean he understood what was best for Kate's family. Still, he had been right about so much, what if he was also right about this? Kate refused to accept that she would one day fail her mother. Even if Jack didn't believe in her ability to take care of them both, she knew her love for her mother would make all things possible. She had no other option.

Jack held his mouth in a straight line as he listened to her. But before he could respond, they heard a shout from inside the barn.

Howard, the old cowboy who also worked on the ranch, came to the open doorway and let out a shrill whistle, then shouted, "Kate, looks like Scarlett is ready to foal early. I think you better come in here and help. She's acting pretty distressed."

Scarlett was a young mare the ranch had rescued from a hoarding situation out in the valley up north. Poor thing had been seriously emaciated when they got her, so all season they'd been working to get her strong enough to carry her foal to term. There should've been more time before Scarlett was ready to give birth. Kate feared there wouldn't be any way to save either of them if things went wrong.

She pushed past Jack, then stopped and turned back. But before she could ask for the favor she needed, he nodded in anticipation.

"Don't worry," he assured her. "I'll go back and check on

Nancy. I can stay for a bit and keep her company if you're going to be a while."

Kate wasn't sure how to say thank you, knowing she hadn't been very considerate to him before when he was trying to help her by offering his professional opinion. Yet he'd immediately known what she needed and had extended his help without question. Having someone else to count on wasn't something she was used to anymore. Not since her mother had begun her sharp cognitive decline.

But she didn't have time to think about what it meant that Jack was so ready and willing to do what he could for them. If he was willing to give her a break so she could tend to Scarlett without worrying about her mom, too, then she was going to take it.

CHAPTER 4

KATE HELD THE TINY FOAL'S HEAD ON HER LAP AS THEY SAT together on the straw-covered floor. She tipped the bottle back so the foal could get the colostrum she desperately needed to give her the best fighting chance at survival.

"Are you in here, Kate?" a voice called out from the door, interrupting the quiet of the early morning barn. The other horses had been turned out already to enjoy some time in the warmth of the sun.

Brenna tiptoed toward them. She'd once been a guest at the ranch but now worked as the head chef here. She did most of the cooking in the main house with some assistance for larger events. In fact, Brenna was one of the first people she'd met when Kate had first come to the ranch. They'd become fast friends, each respecting the other enough not to ask too many probing, hurtful questions.

Thankfully, things seemed to be working out nicely for Brenna these days. She'd come to terms with many of the things that had happened in her past and was now moving forward in a relationship with a man she loved. And the best part was that there was no doubt how much her new beau Matt loved Brenna in return.

"Come say hello to our new arrival," Kate said softly, trying not to startle the little thing. Still, the filly stopped sucking and turned her soft head to glance at Brenna's approaching form. Hunger must have overtaken curiosity because she quickly went back to sucking on the bottle Kate held out for her.

"I heard Scarlett had her foal last night. A bit early, wasn't it?" Brenna talked quietly as she crouched down on the straw beside them.

"It was. I'm worried about her. She's so small and weak, and Scarlett's still frightened and confused. Unfortunately, she rejected her foal, so now it's up to us to nurse the poor dear to health. It's going to be a long road for her."

"All long roads lead to Memory Ranch, it seems." Brenna reached out and stroked the dark chestnut fur. "Poor little thing. I'm not surprised that Scarlett rejected her, though. She's young and weak herself, and this is her first foal. She probably knows she can't offer what this little girl needs."

Kate nodded and smiled sadly. "I know. I was just hoping there would be a better outcome." She'd been wishing that a lot lately, especially when it came to mothers and daughters. "Scarlett has been through so much and now this little one will be in for a fight, too. It just doesn't seem fair."

"No, it doesn't. But at least she has one thing going for her. She has you in her corner, and I know you'll do everything you can to help her."

Kate laughed softly. "You're right about that. I just hope it's going to be enough."

Brenna widened her eyes and grabbed Kate by the shoulder. "That should be her name."

"What should?" Kate studied her friend in confusion.

Brenna beamed with the excitement that came with a great idea. *"Hope.* That's what you should call her. If there's anything I've learned in these past few months, hope is the one thing that can keep you going when all else feels lost. And you know Memory Ranch gives hope to all who come here. Maybe this little girl could become a symbol of that for all of us."

Kate's eyes fell on the weak animal lying in the straw beside her. Right now, it didn't look good for her. The road ahead wound uphill and would be undoubtedly be filled with bumps and sudden turns. Maybe Kate needed hope just as much as the foal in her arms.

Yes, Brenna was right.

"That's a pretty tall order for such a tiny filly. But I think it's perfect." Kate leaned forward and whispered loudly into the filly's ear. "How do you like your new name, Hope?"

The large brown eyes that seemed out of place on her tiny head opened widely, and Kate was almost sure certain saw a spark of strength light from within.

Maybe Hope could get through this, after all.

For her part, Kate would do everything she could to make sure of it.

They sat for a few minutes in silence, listening to the sound of sucking as Hope drained the last of her colostrum. Would it be enough? Had they gotten it to her on time?

Newborn foals needed the colostrum from their mothers to help fight off the bacteria and infections that could affect them later on. But since Hope had been rejected by Scarlett, she hadn't received the vital nourishment. Thankfully, they always had some frozen to keep on hand for emergencies like this.

Kate pictured the baby horse growing strong and frolicking in the yard. If she wished for it hard enough, perhaps she could make it a reality.

"So, I came down here with an ulterior motive in mind." Brenna pulled her knees up to hug to her chest as she peeked over at her friend.

"Uh oh. What's up?" Kate asked as she stroked the now sleeping Hope.

"Howard told me that you'd been out here nonstop since

late last night. It's my job to relieve you and to tell you to go get some breakfast."

Kate shook her head, and the sudden dizziness made her realize just how tired she had allowed herself to become. "I'll go, but not to eat. I've got to get back to my cabin and check on Mom."

Brenna's eyes lighted with the promise of more good news to come. "No need. Doctor Jack actually got her up to the main house for breakfast."

Kate's voice cracked. "Really?"

"Yeah, he stayed with her all night since you were tied up here with Hope. He's a good guy, that one."

She nodded even though she now felt worse about her last interaction with Jack. She hadn't been the nicest and he'd still gone above and beyond for her mother.

Scarlett whinnied from the stall next to them, so Kate pulled herself to her feet to go check on her. She slowly stepped away from the sleeping Hope, careful not to move her.

Brenna stood, too, and reached down to brush the straw from her pants. "And also, before you head up to the house, I have a second ulterior motive this morning. It's ...well..." She held her hand out toward Kate, and it took her a moment to notice a fresh tattoo on her ring finger.

Kate's breath caught in her throat. She'd never seen

Brenna so excited about anything. "Is that...? Are you...? You're getting married! Oh, Brenna, I'm so happy for you."

She grabbed her friend and pulled her in for a hug. "When? How?"

They both laughed as Kate's voice gushed with excitement.

"Last night. And Matt said he doesn't want to wait. Neither do I. We've both spent so long running away from things, so we decided to finally run toward something. *Together.*"

Kate grinned as she took another look at the ornate tattoo band. "Why am I not surprised?" Everyone on the ranch had witnessed the love blossom between Brenna and Matt. They'd gotten off to a rocky start, but by the time they finally admitted what they felt for each other, there was no doubt in anyone's minds that the two would be getting married—and soon.

Brenna confirmed this as she jumped headlong into detailing her plans for Kate. "So, we're getting married in the spring, right here on the ranch. We're going to use the old barn where the dances are held. And, Kate, I want you to be my maid of honor."

It took a few seconds for her to register what Brenna had just said, but when she did, her eyes slowly lifted and met her friend's. Kate was the first person Brenna had let in after years of hiding her abusive home life from everyone outside her family. The fact she'd come so far toward recovery, well, it meant that anything was possible. Perhaps even a miracle for her mother—and for their new Hope as well.

"Please?" Brenna begged. "It would mean the world to me. Then you can help me pull everything together on time."

Kate could only nod and pull Brenna for another hug. She was too emotional, too tired, from so much good and bad all at once it made her head spin.

Brenna laughed. "I take it that's a yes?"

"Yes, Brenna. I'd love to stand beside you at your wedding."

In fact, it was the one thing she was looking forward to most right now. Because if there was one thing she could count on, it was that Brenna and Matt had been made for each other and that their wedding would be a beautiful occasion.

CHAPTER 5

A FEW MORNINGS LATER, KATE FOUND HERSELF SITTING across the table from her mother in what was becoming a welcome new tradition.

"I'm so happy for Brenna," her mom said, skewering a sausage link with her fork. "She seems like such a nice girl. I wasn't quite sure what to think of Matt when I met him. I mean, all those tattoos. But he's proven to be a very nice man, and I think he'll give Brenna a great life."

Kate smiled as she recalled the conversation with her friend. That had been the first day she and her mother had eaten breakfast together at the big house, and in the days that had followed they hadn't yet broken their streak. Each day, Kate rose early to check on Hope, then circled back to the cabin to collect her mother for group breakfast.

So far, so good.

The little filly was hanging on, but each new day brought new challenges to her survival. A newborn foal required frequent feedings, which meant all the ranch hands took turns and rotated shifts when it came to nurturing Hope.

Luckily, her mother had become almost as excited for the wedding as Brenna and Matt themselves, which gave Kate a safe topic to discuss with her during their meals.

"They're going to get married in the spring, so that's not going to leave much time to plan," she confided. "Brenna says she doesn't want anything fancy, so I won't need to spend a fortune on a bridesmaid dress I'll never wear again. I'm just going to find something simple and pretty that I will get more use out of."

Her mom glanced up from her scrambled eggs with a blank expression on her face. "Why are you buying a dress, dear?" she asked earnestly.

A familiar stabbing pain erupted in Kate's chest whenever her mom forgot things. She tried not to let her worry show as she answered, "It's for Brenna's wedding, Mom. She's getting married in the spring, and I'm going to be her maid of honor."

"Oh, that's wonderful. She's such a nice girl." The gigantic grin that spread across her mother's face proved she was receiving this news for the first time in her memory.

The scariest part was that she didn't even know she'd forgotten something.

Kate looked down at her own plate, hoping her mom wouldn't be able to see the pain in her eyes. If she noticed her daughter was upset, it wouldn't take long for her to recognize why. That often led to panic, anger, tantrums. Kate just couldn't handle it. Not right now. Not today.

"Yes, she's been a good friend. I'm happy for her," she said, forcing a smile of her own.

"What's wrong, Kate? You seem upset." Her mom's voice held the same loving concern it always had. All these years she'd strived to protect her daughter, to keep her happy, but she had no idea that now she was the one causing Kate pain.

She lifted her gaze back up to her mom and smiled. They'd been enjoying the chance to sit and talk over breakfast like they'd done so often when Kate was growing up. For a brief moment she'd allowed herself to forget everything had changed. Why had she taken all those breakfasts before for granted? Why hadn't she recorded more details for her own memory? Why hadn't she known how special they were? How much she'd one day yearn for them?

She wrapped both hands around her glass of orange juice and shrugged. "Nothing, Mom. I think I'm just tired from spending so much time working with Hope yesterday."

"Who is Hope? Is she another friend of yours?" Her mother smiled broadly, completely unaware of the fact Kate had discussed Hope with her several times since the baby horse had been born. The moment she had been dreading was upon them now.

This was it.

Things would never be normal for them again.

This was her new normal.

"No, she's a little foal who was born early. She's not very healthy and her mom has rejected her, so we're having to nurse her back to health." Maybe if she just gave a few details it would all come rushing back. This could just be a temporary lapse, a false alarm. It didn't have to mean everything was changing. *Please don't let it mean that everything is changing.*

The older woman's brow pinched with concern. "Oh, the poor little thing. I'd love to come out and see her. I've always loved horses."

Kate reached out and patted her mom's hand. "How about after breakfast I take you out to meet her? I know you'd love her." She knew because they'd already met several times before. How could Hope have fallen right out of her brain?

Her mom's face lit up with excitement. "I'm ready whenever you are." She set her fork down and wiped her mouth with the cloth napkin by her plate. Kate looked down at the nearly full plate and shook her head.

She couldn't stop the sigh that escaped her. "You've

hardly eaten anything. We only just sat down a few minutes ago."

Her mom scrunched her features in confusion as she regarded the plate before her. "Haven't I?" Her voice sounded worried and small, one of those moments where she knew she'd done something that wasn't right. It was always better for them both when her mom didn't realize she'd forgotten.

The times like this—where she knew she was failing and remembered why—they broke Kate in a way nothing else could.

"It's okay. There's no hurry. Besides I'm so hungry, I could eat a... zebra." She tried to make light of the mishap to spare her mother's feelings. But she knew it was too late to shield her from the angst that followed a memory lapse like this one. Soon she'd be back in bed and refuse to leave for the rest of the day, no matter how hard Kate tried to convince her otherwise.

Her mother pushed her plate to the side and frowned. "I guess I'm just not really that hungry."

Kate recognized the fear in her eyes. She had to swallow the lump that formed in her throat from knowing there was nothing she could do to make her mom feel better.

"Mind if I sit with you?" Jack interrupted, coming up beside their table. "I was just going to grab a muffin and head back to my office, but I figured sitting down with company was better than staring at the wall over my desk."

He looked back and forth between them, his smile slowly fading. "Is everything all right here?"

While Kate contemplated the best answer, her mother rushed to explain, "I'm just forgetting so much today already." Her eyes filled with tears and she quickly reached up to wipe at them, putting a brave smile on her face when she glanced back to Kate.

"It's okay, Nancy. We talked about this." Jack sat down on the chair beside her mom and put his hand on hers while he put his other arm around her shoulders.

Kate watched and realized with a sudden jolt just how frail her mom had become during these last few weeks. It almost seemed to have happened overnight.

She felt Jack's gaze fall upon her and glanced up just in time to catch his reassuring smile before he turned back to her mother and spoke in hushed whispers.

"You're going to have some bad days, but you can still look forward to and enjoy the good ones. I mean, you're still able to sit here and visit with your daughter and enjoy a nice meal together. Not to mention the fact you have a hand-some, charming man stopping by to say hello. That's got to count for something, doesn't it?" He grinned down at her mom who rolled her eyes in response.

Slowly the storm was breaking, the clouds were parting, and the sun would be coming out to make everything better again.

"Let me know when the handsome man is coming by, won't you, Jack?" her mother said with a chuckle. "But you're right. I'm grateful I still have the time to spend with Kate. I just hope I don't ever do anything to embarrass her too badly."

Kate's mouth dropped open and she shook her head adamantly. "Mom, there's nothing you could do to ever embarrass me. Well, at least not any worse than that time you drove me to junior high in your pajamas and jumped out of the car to chase me down when I forgot my lunch in the car."

Her mom's laugh became stronger, more robust, and it made Kate feel so much better to hear the joy in it. "You were furious with me. I remember you liked that boy, what was his name…?"

Her mom looked sideways as she struggled to remember. "Peter! Peter Whalens. And Peter was standing next to the door holding it for you when I finally caught up to you." Her mom leaned forward as she laughed at the memory.

Kate's body relaxed as her mother recounted the story for Jack. It seemed so strange that her mom could remember every little detail about an event many years in the past but struggled to recall things Kate had told her just a few minutes prior. But then again, everything about this illness seemed strange.

How her mom could seem physically fine while so many

37

things were breaking within. How a relatively young woman could come be transformed by a disease that normally only preyed on the elderly. How they'd both ended up here, and this was their life now.

She watched as Jack laughed with her mom. There was something about him that just seemed to set her mother at ease. She was so glad he'd shown up when he did, because he'd managed to free her mother from the growing panic and bring back her smile.

"You know, Nancy," Jack said as he wiped his mouth with a napkin. "I think maybe we should start our session a little early today. Since you seem to be done with breakfast already, that is."

Kate's mom blinked and glanced down at her empty plate with a surprised giggle. "Oh, would you look at that. I guess I am."

Jack stood and gathered all their plates for a quick trip to the sink. "Kate, will you be joining us today?"

"No, I've got to get out to the stables to take care of our premature filly." Kate watched the effortless way he interacted with her mother and felt a small stab of jealousy. *Ridiculous.* They were both so lucky to have him. She couldn't let herself forget that.

Jack returned and kept his eyes focused on her mother but spoke to Kate. "Oh, right, you named her Hope, right?"

"Yeah and if she's going to have any hope, I'd better get out there and see what the vet has to say."

"Well, this doc says good luck. Nancy, shall we?" He offered his arm to Kate's mom in a move that reminded Kate of an old-fashioned knight. Her mother rolled her eyes again before standing up.

Kate paused for a moment to watch her mother walk off with Jack, animatedly recounting another time she'd managed to embarrass Kate. Shaking her head part with relief and part with exhaustion, she slipped into her jacket and jogged across the field to the stables.

CHAPTER 6

NORMALLY THE STABLES WERE MOSTLY EMPTY WHEN KATE worked with the horses, but today it was filled with residents and other staffers of the ranch all wanting to see what the veterinarian would say about Hope and her chances.

Kate pushed herself to the front of the group. The vet's grim expression as he stood next to Old Howard sent her heart galloping within her chest.

"What's up, Doc?" she asked, cringing to herself at the bad joke.

The doctor cleared his throat before speaking. "Well, I was just telling the others that we can take Hope into the clinic and keep her there for the next few days to see what we can do. But to be honest, I don't think she'd get anymore care there than she's already getting here. You've been doing a great job nursing her along."

Kate kept her eyes on the sick filly lying in the straw.

"Unfortunately, it's not all great news," the vet continued. "Hope didn't get colostrum right away, so I'm pretty certain she's suffering from neonatal sepsis. It's common in foals that didn't have a good start in life. I've given her a shot of antibiotics to get her started, but you can carry on with her treatment here. She will need a lot of fluids and some TLC over the next few days. I should have the bloodwork back in a day or so and then we'll know for sure what we're dealing with."

Old Howard pushed his hat back on his head. "There's something else we need to keep in mind, too. The weatherman says we're due to get some snow dumped on us out here and the roads very well might wind up closed. So whatever we do, we've gotta commit to the next few days being stuck with it. If we keep her here and something comes up, we may not have any way to get help."

"What do you think, Kate?" her boss and ranch owner, Elizabeth Jane, asked. "You're the one who's closest to Hope. Should we let the doc take her back into town now before the roads all close? Or are going to keep her here?"

Elizabeth Jane, Howard, and the doctor looked at her nervously, waiting for her opinion. None of them wanted to make what could be a life-or-death decision for the young foal, and none of them wanted to take the right to decide away from Kate. They all knew how much she'd come to care about Hope over the past few days.

Kate reached down to stroke the filly as she spoke. "I think she should stay here. I wouldn't feel right knowing she was all alone overnight in a strange place. I can try staying with her all night somehow. It's just..."

Elizabeth came over and put her arm around Kate's shoulders. "I know this is a difficult situation, and I know it's hard dealing with this kind of setback when you've given so much to Hope. If it would help, I can call the respite service and ask for them to send someone out right away before the storm gets too bad. They can stay in the cabin with Nancy, so you don't have to worry."

Kate let out a breath she hadn't even realized she'd been holding. "That would be great. Thank you so much. I'll just need to talk to my mom about what's happening first."

The vet shuffled around in his portable trunk and pulled out a small package, extending it toward Kate. "Continue with the treatment as we discussed earlier and keep me updated. I'll call you as soon as I have the results back. Now, I need to get going before I get caught in this storm, too."

"Thanks for coming, Doctor Cooper." She shook his hand, then turned to go into the stall and check on Hope again.

Elizabeth's arm fell away but she followed Kate to the center of the stall. "I'll go call the respite service now. Don't worry about your mom. Even if they can't get someone out here, I will gladly spend the night with her so that you can keep an eye on Hope. I think you made the right call, by the way." Liz smiled at her sadly. They both knew what was at stake here.

"I do, too," Brenna said, saddling Kate with a quick hug. "I wish I could stay here with you, but I have to get back to my kitchen."

"Go, go, both of you," Kate urged. "You have plenty to do to get ready for the storm. Hope and I will be fine on our own."

As the last of the crowd dispersed, Kate eyed the swirling whiteness on the other side of the barn door. The late winter storm had already started to build. They didn't have much time before the worst of it was upon them.

What if Hope did end up getting worse and they couldn't get her to the vet? Her life was literally in Kate's hands now, and the responsibility of it weighed heavily on her shoulders.

It was a different battle than what she was dealing with in her mom's case because, no matter how hard she fought for her mom, the disease would ultimately win. But if she gave her all to the little horse, she could make a real difference.

Kate had the power to save Hope's life. She'd fallen hopelessly in love with the fragile animal, and she would do anything to help her. The renewed sense of purpose sent warmth flickering through her. It seemed this little horse was helping her as much as she was helping it.

"I'll leave you to care for our wee little filly here, Kate," Howard said, pulling his gloves back on. Kate hadn't even realized he'd stayed behind when the others left.

"I've got to round up the rest of the horses outside and get them in from the storm. I'll be back to check on you in a bit." Howard gave her a kind smile before turning to leave. He was one of the oldest cowboys working on the ranch and she had quickly learned he was a big softie. Without a doubt he would be the one other person who'd worry about Hope as much as she was.

Kate leaned back against a bale at the back of the stall and placed her arms on her bent knees. She watched the gentle rise and fall of Hope's chest with every difficult breath she took.

How many times in a day did she have to say to herself that something wasn't fair? Lately it seemed as though everything in her life was a series of painful experiences which, if she believed all of the self-help books she'd read over the years, were supposed to make her grow.

Even though Hope had only been born less than a week ago, she had begun to gain strength in her knock-kneed legs. But then the sepsis set in, erasing all the progress they'd made. How much more could the horse's small body endure?

How much more could Kate endure?

Her mind drifted back to her mom and Jack. Over the past week, her mother had gone to visit Jack a couple more times and, just like today, he'd asked if she wanted to join. If it hadn't been for Hope today, she might've finally given in. Still, Kate could sense that her mom didn't want her there any more than Kate wanted to go, so she normally found an excuse to avoid a shared session.

They both already knew the truth—and the eventual outcome—of their situation. Sitting and talking about it together just didn't seem like it would do anything to help either of them. Of course, the private sessions with Jack were greatly improving her mom's morale, and someday Kate would have to thank him for the kindness and compassion he'd shown her. But that didn't mean she needed to force herself into a situation where she was not fully welcome.

She needed to respect her mother's wishes, even if she didn't fully understand them yet.

Besides, Jack's job was to help however he could, and if her mother didn't want Kate to be a part of her treatment, then he couldn't force it. Even with this limitation, he gave her mother and the patients his all, taking his care well beyond the normal obligations of a therapist. Such was the powerful draw of the ranch. They truly had something special here, and Kate just didn't know what she'd have done without it.

She pulled her knees in to her chest and rested her chin on them. For a few brief moments, she let her mind wander to the therapist who she had to admit had somehow snuck his way into her dreams at night. It seemed so funny since she'd known him now for a few months, but they'd only really spoken more since her mom moved in and started seeing him.

Whether it was taking his meals at the big house or walking the paths near the barn, he seemed to turn up every-where she went these days.

This was the worst possible time and the worst possible circumstance for her to develop a crush—and she could *never* act on her feelings—but every once in a while she let herself imagine *what if?*

What if we'd met under different circumstances?

What if Mom had never gotten sick?

What if Jack harbored secret feelings for her, too?

What if? What if? What if?

But, no. Not only was Jack too ethical to ever fall for a patient's caregiver, he was also far out of her league. He had good looks, good brains, a good heart, and Kate was as average as they came. She had never stood out in a crowd. In fact, she usually tried to stay in the background where no one would notice her. She'd had a few boyfriends over the years, but never anything long-term that made her face light up like Brenna's did when she was with Matt.

Kate shook these daydreams from her head and crawled over to lay down beside Hope in the straw. Her body was tired, and the strain of the past few weeks with her mom and now with the premature foal took over. She decided to rest her eyes for a moment, knowing she could trust Elizabeth Jane to take good care of her mother in the interim.

As her eyes closed, she let herself imagine being held in the warmth of a strong embrace. Jack's face smiled down at her as he stroked her hair and told her she would never be alone.

It would never be her reality, but at least she could dream.

CHAPTER 7

"Kate," a muffled voice called, rousing her from sleep. Slowly she blinked her eyes open and stretched her arms to the side.

Jack's image came into focus as he called her name again. "Kate?"

No, this must still be a dream. She'd never be awakened by Jack in real life. He'd never call her name so tenderly.

His warm fingers caressed her cheek, and in that moment it felt so unbelievably real. Then, that handsome smile of his contorted in a frown as he began to back away.

No, don't go. I'm not ready to wake up and go back to the real world...

"Kate, I think Hope needs you," Jack said a bit louder than before.

Hope...Hope!

That did it. She rubbed the sleep from her eyes and gave herself a pinch for good measure. Jack stood across the stall, studying her. It was Hope who lay beside her, breathing hot, labored puffs onto Kate's cheek.

She struggled to sit up without rousing the foal. She tried her best to compose herself, embarrassed that Jack, of all people, had been the one to catch her sleeping on the job.

He knelt forward and offered her both hands to help pull her to her feet.

Kate clasped them tightly but immediately wished she hadn't as an electric jolt ricocheted right through her. As soon as she was back to a standing position, she let go of Jack and busied herself by wiping all the errant straw from her clothes.

Jack just smiled and waited for her to be done. "I walked Nancy back to your cabin after our session," he explained. "When the respite worker there said she hadn't seen you since she'd arrived, I figured you'd be here.

"And look," he said, his eyes glinting playfully. "It seems I was right."

"Is everything okay?" Kate's eyes darted around the barn in search of danger. But all the horses were tucked peacefully into their stalls, which meant she had slept for quite a while and quite soundly, too, since she'd managed not to wake while the horses were stabled for the night.

"Relax," he told her. "Everything's fine. Nancy was a bit

tired, but that's to be understood. She's getting along great with the respite worker and even asked if I would find you and let you know that you didn't need to rush home on her account."

Kate sighed heavily. "I just feel like I've been neglecting her more in past few days since Hope was born. I've been so busy here at the barn that I haven't been able to do much else."

Jack shook his head and leaned against the wall of the pen. "You have a job to do and she understands that. You can't spend every waking hour with her, no matter how much you want to. That simply isn't possible."

Kate moved to the edge of the stall to prepare formula for Hope, who was becoming restless as she awaited her meal. Her legs were too weak to stand, but it didn't stop her from trying as she moved around in the straw beneath her. When Kate had the bottle ready, she crouched back down and let Hope lift her head to drink like she would from her mother.

With Hope taken care of, Kate returned to the topic of her mother. "Maybe you're right, but I still should be spending as much time as I can now. It's not like I've got the rest of my life to hang out with her. I need to be there for her while she still remembers me."

Jack crouched down beside her, his dark eyes boring into hers. He wasn't dressed in his usual office attire, and that made Kate wonder if something had changed, something important she didn't know about yet.

Today he wore denim, a better kept version of what the cowboys who worked in the stables wore—sans holes, patches, dirt, and otherwise worn-in spots. She had to admit the crisp denim suited him well. Made him more approachable, too.

"I can understand feeling that way, Kate," he said, putting a hand on her shoulder. "But you'll only make yourself crazy trying to do it all. I mean, look at what you're doing right now. You're working full time here at the ranch, you've got this little horse here to care for, and you're trying to be Nancy's full-time caregiver, too. As much as I know you don't want to admit it, something has to give. And if you don't pick where to cut back, life is going to choose for you."

He searched her eyes as if checking to see if his words had stuck. "Just enjoy your time with her when you *are* together. Time is the one thing that is never guaranteed. It's something you can't force, either. Believe me, I know."

She knew he was right and that he spoke from professional experience. Still, it felt wrong not to be with her mother every second she could manage. She already felt torn between Hope and her mother, and guilty that someone else had to be called in to tend to her mother.

"I try to tell myself that, but it's hard."

Jack eyed her seriously. "Well, not to sound like a broken

record, but if you'd come to a therapy session with your mom, we could likely talk about some of these things."

He chuckled when she lifted her head to argue with him. "I know, I know. But a guy has to at least try where he can!"

She hesitated before saying, "It's not that I don't want to..."

"But you're just not sure how much it will help." He laughed again as he finished her sentence. "I get it. And I'm not going to push you. I'm fine just talking to you as a friend. If I can help you even a little bit, then that's all I need."

She glanced down at Hope, who was making good progress with her bottle. "Talking about it with you, with her, it just makes it all so real, you know? I know she's declining. And I know I'm going to have to make some hard decisions soon... I'm just not ready yet."

Kate watched as Hope sucked hard on the bottle. She hoped that the strength of her sucking was a good sign, but she also knew this first night was going to be crucial before the antibiotic had a chance to start working. She let Hope finish off the bottle and rubbed her neck as she pulled it away. Hope lay her head in the straw, her big brown eyes watching Kate's every move. Even with the good meal in her, the horse was still far too weak from the infection.

"What's going to happen with her?" Jack asked gently.

It took Kate a moment to figure out whether he was

talking about the filly or about her mother. When he reached out to pet Hope with soft, slow strokes, she knew.

She closed her eyes and tried to picture Hope strong and healthy, but the image wouldn't come. Opening her eyes again, she confided, "She's pretty sick, but I'm hoping that if I can get her through tonight, she'll at least have a fighting chance. Since the respite worker is here for my mom, I'm going to spend the night down here in the barn and keep a close eye on Hope. I have to do whatever it takes to help her."

A smile spread across Jack's face as he shifted his gaze to Kate. "You're a good person, Kate. And, lucky for you— perhaps lucky for the both of us—I'm stuck out here at the ranch for the night, so you'll have some company."

Heat rushed to Kate's cheeks. He considered himself lucky to spend time with her? No, she must have misunderstood.

"I don't think you need to stay here, too," she hedged. "Besides, it's not like you would be able to do much to help anyway." Her insides warred as to whether his company would be welcome that evening.

He rolled his eyes as he pulled himself back to his full height. "I'll have you know that just because I'm a therapist, it doesn't mean I don't know anything about horses. Do you think I just fell into a job on the ranch? I grew up around horses and probably know my way around a barn just as well as any of the cowboys working here."

Her mouth fell open she tried to think of what else she could say here.

But Jack raised his hand to stop her. "You go ahead and check on your mom. I'll stay here with Hope until you get back. Then I'll head up to the house and grab us something to eat."

Her mouth still hung open, but words wouldn't come. Even if she could think of a legitimate way to put him off, she sensed Jack wouldn't back down.

Not this time.

Not about this.

In fact, he'd already pulled his jacket off and settled down onto a bale of hay, waiting for her to get going. Kate couldn't tell him she needed him to leave because she really had no good reason to make him. And that little part of her in the far corner of her heart might just want him to stay after all.

CHAPTER 8

SPENDING ALL DAY TUCKED AWAY IN THE STABLES WITH Hope caused Kate to lose track of time. She sat with Hope and stroked her muzzle as the horse dozed between feedings. The antibiotics would be coursing through her now, strengthening her immune system so she could fight off this nasty infection.

Caring for the little foal seemed so straightforward.

Get sick, take medicine, get better.

If only everything were this simple.

Perhaps one day scientists would discover a cure for Alzheimer's. It could save so many others from the slow pain of losing a loved one even before death. Others, but not Kate and her mother. By the time they found a cure, her mother would have already lost her fight.

Would she be in Heaven looking down?

Kate refused to think of any other possibility. Someday soon her mom would be living in eternal paradise. Kate would be the one who'd need to forge a way on her own as she fought the bleak world left behind.

These thoughts were interrupted by a cold breeze as Jack pushed through the stable door, his arms loaded with small bags. "Hey," he whispered as he sat down next to her. "I hope you're hungry, because I've got two containers of stew, a couple roast beef sandwiches, some fresh buns, and some donuts... Those came courtesy of Brenna. And, the *piece de resistance*, a jumbo thermos of coffee."

He wiggled his eyebrows as he lifted the shiny metal thermos high into the air like some kind of holy relic.

Kate took one of the bags from his hands, chuckling at his goofy gesture. "I would have been fine with just the coffee and donuts. You know that, right?" she said, but she already had one of the sandwiches unwrapped and her stomach leapt with anticipation.

"Yeah, uh-huh." He smirked and set the thermos on the ground beside the bale they'd decided to use as their seat. "I would have been, too, because let's be honest, donuts are pretty much my favorite food ever. But Brenna insisted we needed some *proper* food, too." He made air quotes around proper and raised his voice in a spot-on impression of their shared friend.

Kate chuckled between bites of her sandwich. How had she not realized how hungry she'd gotten until now?

Jack watched her eat with a far-off smile on his face. "They're having a bit of a campfire jamboree up at the house. I guess that's a good way to ride out the storm, and I think Brenna might've mentioned that she would run some s'mores out to us when they got to that part of the festivities."

"You know," she said, forcing herself to slow down so she wouldn't get a stomachache from speed eating. "I'm starting to suspect that Elizabeth Jane and Dorian don't improve the roads specifically so they can get snowed in."

"Maybe." Jack chuckled and finally reached into the bag for a donut. "I'm afraid I wasn't able to grab regular silverware, so hopefully plastic sporks and knives will do."

She fought back a surge of embarrassment. Truth be told, she hadn't planned on using any silverware. But maybe it would be better if she didn't slurp stew straight from the container when seated beside a sophisticated man like Jack.

"It's perfect," she murmured appreciatively. "Thank you. I really haven't been eating very well the past few days. Trust me, this meal looks like heaven. Tastes like it, too," she added, realizing she was already half done before Jack had even gotten the chance to start.

He devoured his donuts in two big bites, then unpacked a container of stew for each of them. Steam wafted into the air the moment Kate lifted the lid, and her stomach immediately rumbled with delightful anticipation. She swallowed hard, hoping he hadn't heard it.

Jack raised an eyebrow and smiled in jest. "Well, I think your stomach will be glad I brought more than donuts."

"Yeah," she said with a nervous laugh, then shoved a heaping spoonful of the thick gravy into her mouth to avoid having to say anything more. *"Oww,"* she cried as her eyes teared from the sudden shock of pain that overwhelmed her mouth.

Jack clucked his tongue and handed her a napkin. "It's still hot, Kate."

She glared at him, bringing her fingers up to press against her burning lips. "You know, with smarts like that, you should be a doctor or something," she teased. At least she'd been able to save face with a good comeback.

Despite her desperation to choke down her food as quickly as possible, sitting here with Jack didn't feel forced or strange like she'd feared. She felt mostly at ease with him, and he seemed to fit in well with the barn. She'd never have guessed at this new laidback side of him, and discovering it now only made her like him more. Her crush on him before had been based mostly on his looks and the kind way he treated her mother, but little by little, she was beginning to learn just how compatible the two of them may actually be.

A tomboy herself, Kate had always been drawn to the

kind of man who would get down in the dirt and be willing to muck out a stall. Now she realized that Jack had secretly been that type of guy all along.

Of course, none of that changed the fact that a relationship between them would be impossible, especially as her mother still required so much extra care.

And even though she enjoyed having his company, she saw the danger in allowing herself to become too friendly with Jack.

She fixed her eyes on the far wall of the barn and said, "You really don't have to stay here, you know. I'm sure Liz would give you a room for the night to save you from having to sleep in the barn."

He bumped her gently with his shoulder. "So it's good enough out here for you but not for me?"

"That's not what I meant," she argued.

He stared at her with a knowing expression and a smile quirking at the outer edges of his mouth.

She shook her head and tried to hide the smile creeping across her own face as well. "Okay, fine. It's what I meant."

He gave her that classic gotcha expression, then shrugged. "I know I have other options, but this is the one I want. I want to be here for Hope, and I want to be here for you, too. With you, I mean." A slight blush rose to the apples of his cheeks and he coughed before popping a spoonful of stew into his mouth. Then he coughed some more when he realized firsthand just how hot it was.

Kate couldn't resist gloating. "It's still hot, Jack."

He grabbed a chunk of bread and took a generous bite. "Eh, who really needs taste buds, right?" he managed to say around the bread.

Kate rolled her eyes before glancing toward Hope, who was sleeping quietly by their feet.

Was he flirting with her, or just trying to be a good friend? Could it be possible that he found himself drawn to her as much as she'd always been drawn to him?

No, she was being ridiculous. She blew a quick series of rapid breaths on her stew before taking another bite. This time it was perfect.

Jack continued to tear at the bread and dip it into his bowl. He nodded toward Hope as he spoke. "So what's the plan for tonight? I heard she was sick, but no one filled me in on the finer details."

Kate took a slow, deep breath. Her heart broke every time she thought about all the possible outcomes for the sweet little horse. "Some of the other guys have been taking turns with me for the past week by coming in to feed Hope throughout the night. But now the vet thinks she has neonatal sepsis. We started her on an antibiotic and we're making sure she's fed and hydrated. She seems to respond the best to me, so until she's feeling better, I wouldn't feel right leaving her with anyone else."

Jack patted Hope's flank reassuringly. "Neonatal sepsis is a rough one," he murmured with a frown before looking back toward Kate. "You sure do take a lot of responsibility onto your shoulders, don't you?"

"I do what's needed. And Hope needs me." She finally turned her head back to meet his gaze. "I could never walk away from someone I care about in their hour of need. It may not make much sense, but it's just who I am."

That was part of the reason she was fighting so hard to keep her mother with her. As long as they were both on the ranch, they could be together. She didn't want to trade that for anything—not even an easier arrangement on her part.

She and Jack ate the rest of their meal in silence, listening to the sounds of the horses stomping and whinnying in their stalls.

A short while later, Jack wiped his mouth with a napkin and reached for a third donut. "Well, just tell me what I can do to help, and I'll do my best."

He held her eye an unnaturally long time, leaving Kate to wonder if his offer of help was just for Hope, just for tonight—or if he might want to help her through all the rest of it, too.

Of course he did. He was her mom's therapist. It was his

job to help people through emotional turmoil, and Kate definitely found herself in turmoil now.

She still couldn't figure out whether his interest in her was purely from a professional standpoint or if he might want more. But as he'd already pointed out several times now, Kate had nothing left to give.

CHAPTER 9

KATE WATCHED AS JACK PULLED THE TREMBLING FOAL DOWN onto his lap. He held onto Hope as she started to struggle, desperately trying to stand up, wanting so much to be strong. Patiently, he whispered soothing words into her ear and leaned into her while stroking her neck.

Kate hated seeing the fear that shone in those big brown eyes. If only there was a way to explain to the little horse that everything would be okay, that Kate would make sure of it. She couldn't know for sure what would happen, but she would make that promise to Hope.

The weakness that had a hold of her tiny body fought hard against the huge, determined spirit inside.

Every creature wants to live, Kate thought. *It's instinct.*

She hadn't quite figured out what that meant for her yet.

When it came to people, did living merely mean surviving—or was it something deeper than that?

She suppressed a yawn as Jack did all the heavy lifting for Hope's care.

He'd stayed to help with the other feedings throughout the night, and she was sure it must be close to three in the morning by now. The schedule was rigorous and brutal, but it's what Hope needed, so it was what Kate would do.

Jack, too, apparently.

If they could just get her through the rest of tonight. Then tomorrow. Through this infection. Through anything else that popped up.

Hope wasn't just a name. Not to Kate. A heavy emotional weight rested on that little horse's shoulders. She meant more to Kate than perhaps she should, especially given the chances she'd survive to adulthood.

No, she couldn't think about that now.

Willing her mind to be blank, she rose to prepare the formula for Hope's next feeding.

A minute later, Jack accepted the bottle and held it up the way he'd seen her doing it, and thankfully Hope latched onto it right away to start sucking. Jack's other hand continued to move up and down the foal's neck in a rhythmic pattern as she ate.

Just a few more hours and they'd all have a better idea of Hope's odds.

"She's going to be a beautiful horse when she grows up," Jack whispered, speaking to Kate but keeping his eyes fixed lovingly on the foal.

Kate sat down cross-legged in the straw beside him. "I sure hope she gets that chance."

Jack continued to smile at the foal as he spoke. "Oh, I recognize something in her eyes. She's going to get that chance. There's a whole lot of fight left in her. Just you wait and see."

Hearing the confidence in his voice eased her own worry just enough to slow her wildly beating heart. If Jack thought Hope would make it, then Kate had could find a way to believe, too.

They sat together without speaking as they listened to the sound of the filly's loud sucking.

Kate let out a little laugh at just how quickly and desperately Hope ate. She seemed to believe Jack's prognosis, too.

"She's got to be feeling better," Jack said, struggling to keep the bottle upright as Hope drank with everything she had. "When I watched her take that first bottle last night she was hardly drinking. Now it's like she can't get it down quick enough."

"Maybe she's just trying to impress you." Kate laughed as glanced toward her with a cocked eyebrow. "You've gotta admit, she does seem pretty smitten with you."

Their coffee and snacks had run out sometime during

the night, but the conversation between them had never faltered as they'd begun to build a comfortable friendship with each other and bonded over the sick filly.

Something about his demeanor relaxed her once she got over the awkwardness of her attraction. His strong, soothing presence was probably what made him such an effective therapist in the first place. That, and he was a good listener. Although he didn't talk much at all about himself, Kate realized.

She scooted closer to him in the hay and said, "You know all about my family, but I don't know anything about yours. So spill it. You told me before you're from around here. What else do I need to know? Do you still have family close by?" *Or a girlfriend,* she silently added, once more cursing the torch she carried for Doctor Jack.

He slid out from under Hope as she finished the bottle and tossed it over to Kate. "Not much to say, really. I grew up in the Valley on a ranch right between Wasilla and Palmer, and well, I never left. Alaska, that is. My apartment and practice is in Anchorage, but I've still got a bunch of family all over the place, so we tend to get together often enough. I have an older sister who is married with two kids. And I have a younger brother, Martin—or Marty, as he insists we call him. He still lives with my folks, but he DJs events around town. He's always loved music and could tell you the title, singer, or even writer of just about every song ever."

He smiled wide before explaining, "He was born with Down Syndrome and he's just about the most inspiring person you could ever meet. He's one of the reasons I became a therapist. I really just wanted to be able to help people the way he does."

"He sounds amazing," she said, placing her hand on his arm, feeling especially close to him now that he'd begun to open up and had shared something so important with her.

Hope grunted in seeming agreement, which sent them both into another fit of shared laughter. They both knelt down next to her and began petting the shaky little horse.

"He is," Jack said thoughtfully. "Growing up I used to get into fights with people who tried to bully him. In high school I got into a brawl with this punk kid who'd been calling Marty all sorts of awful things. I just couldn't take it anymore, so I did something about it. Of course, then I got suspended for two weeks because of how I decided to handle it."

He laughed to himself as he remembered his formative years. "Well, the very next day, Marty came into my room and told me I shouldn't have been fighting because it wasn't a nice thing to do. I told him sometimes you have to fight for the people you love and for the people who aren't able to fight for themselves. I didn't tell him that he was both and that I'd thrown that first punch to defend him, but what he told me next changed my entire life."

Kate sucked in a deep breath. "What was it?"

Jack had a far-off smile on his face. "Marty just shook his head and said, 'No, you don't have to fight. Teach them to be nicer instead.'" His eyes dropped to their hands on Hope's neck. "It was such a simple concept, but it changed me from that day on."

"He sounds like a wise person everyone could learn a lot from."

Jack lifted his eyes and smiled. "I'd like you to meet him sometime. I've been thinking about bringing him out to see the ranch. He loves animals, has since he was little. In fact, he still helps to take care of the horses and other livestock back home. I think he'd love Hope."

"Well, then you should bring him out. Sounds like he might do wonders for Hope's spirit, too." *And maybe even mine,* she thought.

Jack's smile faded. "So you're not worried about having him around Hope? I mean, I know he's very gentle and would never hurt an animal, but sometimes people don't know what to think about him and that can make him seem dangerous."

"Absolutely not," Kate said, shaking her head. "I think Marty sounds wonderful and I'd love to have him around the animals here. Especially Hope."

Jack let out a relieved sigh. Even now he seemed protective of his little brother. "Thank you for letting me tell you about Marty," he said. "He's such an important part of who I am that sometimes it feels dishonest that everyone doesn't know."

Kate nodded. She felt the exact same way about her mom even before she'd fallen sick.

As Hope finally settled down and started sleeping again, Kate brushed a bit of stray hair from her long face. "I know I was resistant at first, but I have to admit, it's been nice having the company. And I appreciate all your help, too. Between this and everything you've been doing for Mom, I don't know how I could ever repay you."

He leaned back on a bale, grinning like a Cheshire Cat.

"Uh-oh," she said in mock alarm. "What did I get myself into?"

"Well, how about you let me take you on a date?" he suggested with a sly grin.

She started coughing loudly, choking on her saliva as she struggled to take in a shaky breath. "You're asking me on a date?" she managed to croak out.

"I'm not sure that's the reaction I was hoping for, but yes. I've had a great time here tonight, getting to know you, trading stories. So, I thought maybe next time we could go somewhere with, I don't know, proper seating? Besides, I still really think you could use a break. Let me give it to you."

The wheels in Kate's mind whirred as she searched frantically for a response. "But you're my mom's therapist. Isn't that against the rules or something?"

He shrugged. "It probably would be if *you* were my patient. But you aren't, and you haven't come to any of your mom's sessions, so I'd say we're smack dab in the middle of a gray area, but I think it's very light gray, if that helps."

"I don't know..." Why was she hesitating? She'd fantasized about just this thing ever since the day she'd first laid eyes on handsome Jack.

"C'mon, it'll be fun. You need some time away from the ranch. I promise I'm a perfect gentleman and I won't make anything awkward or uncomfortable for you. Just a couple friends going out and having some fun."

Her head and her heart were in a brutal battle of wills as she sat and stared at him. All her life she'd let her head do the thinking and pushed away anything that wasn't completely practical. But she realized right now she desperately wanted to listen to her heart.

And the way his deep brown eyes bored into hers made her want to put her brain to bed. Despite all the many reasons why she should turn down his invitation, this time Kate would listen to her heart.

CHAPTER 10

KATE STOOD BACK AND WAITED AS THE TINY FOAL STOOD ON shaky legs, nudging one hoof forward hesitantly in her attempt to reach Kate who stood just a few yards away.

"You can do it, Hope. C'mon girl. Just a few steps and you'll be here."

It had been two days since Jack and Kate had stayed with her overnight, and every hour the horse had been gaining new strength. With her infection beaten, the next hurdle she had to overcome was learning to walk. She'd already managed a few slow steps with Kate's help, and it was time for Hope to attempt the feat based solely on her own strength.

Kate had guided her out of the stall to allow for more space to practice, and now they stood in the barn as a few of the other horses watched from their pens. Their large, sparkly eyes remained glued to Hope, and Kate knew they were rooting for the little one, too. Their gentleness and passion as they focused on the foal warmed Kate's heart. Hope had so many people—and animals—on her team. She just had to make it.

The foal's wobbly legs click-clacked an uneven rhythm as she moved slowly toward Kate. Hope's head swayed gently from side to side as she took in the big, new world outside her stall. The windows behind her illuminated her shadow, and the sunlight glimmered off the deep brown of her coat.

The other horses brayed and snorted, offering their encouragement to the little filly. And while Hope was definitely much better than she had been a few days ago, she still had a long way to go. But slowly, she was getting there.

As she got closer, Hope's gait became steadier. Her legs didn't wobble quite as much now as the muscles learned what they needed to do. Upon reaching Kate, her tail whipped up in excitement almost like she couldn't believe it, either.

Kate laughed and reached out to let the tiny body lean into her. Hope's head pushed into her and rested on her shoulder as Kate wrapped her arms around her neck. "Oh, Hope. I knew you could do it. I wish Jack was here to see this. He'd be so happy."

Just then, Brenna walked around the corner of a stall from behind her.

Kate stood up and proudly pointed at Hope. "Look at my girl. She's almost ready to run the derby."

Brenna laughed and came over to put her hand out for Hope to sniff in greeting. They were all careful not to overwhelm the foal with too much too soon, but the horse herself was eager for more now that she had discovered so much more existed in the world outside her stall.

"I know, look at her!" Brenna cooed as she petted Hope. "Jack couldn't stop telling everyone about how she's standing on her own now, and I knew I just had to see for myself. The way he talks about her you'd think Hope is his child. Yours, too, for that matter."

Kate's cheeks burned. "Well, he's been coming down to check on her a lot. And he really did help during the sepsis scare that had her in such rough shape."

Brenna put her hands up and smiled conspiratorially. "You don't need to explain anything to me. I know Jack loves her. I mean, who wouldn't? But surely you must also know there's something more behind his frequent visits to the barn. Something that starts with a *K* and ends with *ate.*"

Kate slowly started to walk back to Hope's stall, letting her follow at her own pace. She chose to ignore Brenna rather than encourage her.

But that wasn't enough to get her friend to drop the subject. "In fact," she said, tilting her voice up at the end. "I do believe he mentioned that you two are going out this weekend."

She whipped her head around to look at Brenna. "He told you that? Is he going around telling everyone?"

"Don't get so defensive, Kate. I had to pry it out of him." Brenna laughed as they reached Hope's stall, then leaned her arms over the top rung of the stall. "I might have been hinting about Jack's newfound interest in the horses and the barn in particular. He knows we are good friends, so I'm sure he figured I was going to find out anyway. I don't think he's going around telling *everyone*."

Kate mixed up some milk replacer in a pail and set it on the floor. She'd been acclimating Hope to drinking from the bucket now that she was steadier on her feet. So far she seemed to be doing well with the transition from the bottle, and Kate was intensely proud of her little girl.

"Do you think I'm making a mistake?" she asked her friend, letting her eyes linger on the filly before turning back to Brenna.

She scrunched up her face in confusion. "A mistake? What are you talking about?"

"I mean, do you think I should cancel? It just seems like there's so much that could go wrong by actually going out on a date with him. I should be with my mom, or with Hope. It's not the best time for me to be dating, especially when the guy is my mother's therapist and a coworker to boot."

They both watched as Hope came over to drink.

Kate felt a fresh wave of panic ready to overtake her. "It's definitely a mistake, isn't it? What was I thinking saying yes?"

Brenna chortled. "No, I don't think you're making a mistake. The only mistake you're making is the fact that you're overthinking everything. Trust me on that, I used to do the same thing with Matt, and all that did is cause strife between us until I was ready to let it go. Tell me this: why don't you deserve the chance to go out and have a good time?"

Kate licked her lips. "Well, my mom..."

Brenna shook her head adamantly. "Nope, that's not going to fly. I don't believe for a second that she wouldn't want you going out and having fun. Do you really, honestly think she would rather you stay by her side every waking moment rather than taking a few well-deserved moments for yourself? Trust me, your mom wants you to be happy. And I'm sure she would like to know you haven't put your life on hold because of her. Even if that's exactly what you *have* been doing until now."

Kate leaned against the wall and crossed her arms over her chest. "I don't know. It just feels like I should be spending my time with her. She needs me right now. I feel like I'm abandoning her."

Brenna pushed away from the side of the stall and came

into the stall beside Kate. "Stop being so hard on yourself. You're not abandoning her by going out for one night. If it makes you feel better, I can go hang out with her while you're out. Although the last time I did that, she walloped me in cribbage pretty bad. *Hmm,* how is your mom at Hearts?"

Kate shrugged. "I don't know. Maybe it won't be that bad."

Brenna gasped. "Bad? Are we talking about the same Doctor Jack Young here? It'll be good. Very, very good. You're going to have a great time, and that's just what you need."

"Now you sound like him," Kate pointed out.

"Yet another point in his favor," her friend said, sticking her tongue out in jest.

It all made sense, but she still felt as if she was abandoning her post by leaving for a full evening away from the ranch. At least during all her time with Hope in the barn she was still near at hand if her mother needed her for anything.

"Fine, I won't cancel," Kate said at last. "But maybe I'll get lucky and he'll forget."

Brenna exploded in laughter. "Oh poor, naïve Kate. That man is crazy for you. I'm not sure anything else has been on his mind. Believe me, he's got something special planned, and you're going to have the time of your life."

Kate worried her lip. Wouldn't it be better for everyone

if she and Jack had a miserable time and were able to tamp out the sparks between them once and for all?

Brenna put a hand on Kate's arm. "Stop worrying so much. Just go and let yourself have fun. Your mom and Hope will still be here when you get back."

Kate knew Brenna was right, but she also worried she'd already fallen so hard for Jack that she'd never be able to get back up again.

CHAPTER 11

A FEW DAYS LATER, A KNOCK AT THE CABIN DOOR SENT KATE scurrying through the room, double and triple checking everything. She brushed at invisible wrinkles on her blouse, unable to look up for fear he'd notice the fire in her cheeks. Even though they'd formed a comfortable friendship the past few days, tonight changed everything—and that made her incredibly nervous. She took a deep breath and opened the door.

Jack stood there sharply dressed in jeans with a plaid scarf tucked into his pea coat. A smile played at the corners of his mouth as he studied her appreciatively.

"You look amazing, Kate," he said, running a hand through his hair and letting loose that stray curl Kate loved so much. "I think this is the first time I've seen you with your hair down."

She stood back to allow him entry, clearing her throat as he passed her. "I don't really have many dressy clothes, so this was the best I could do," she explained without meeting his eye.

"Well, your best is pretty darn good," Jack said with that ubiquitous smile.

"I hope so since you wouldn't tell me where we're going. For all I know we could just as easily be headed for ballroom dancing as we could be skydiving."

"It's neither of those," he informed her with a chuckle.

She was embarrassed that she only had a good pair of denim jeans to wear, unless she wanted to pull out her one pair of dress pants she used for funerals and weddings. But Jack had told her jeans would be perfectly acceptable for their date when she'd mentioned it.

Of course, she'd tried more than once to find out where they were headed to make sure her casual look wouldn't be out of place. Jack had assured her that anything she chose to wear would be fine, which wasn't really helpful at all. At least she had a couple of nice blouses she'd been able to choose from.

As for her hair, leaving it down had been her mother's idea, even though Kate herself felt very self-conscious about the change from her normal style. She didn't know the first thing about taming her frizz, but her mother had helped with that, too.

They'd had a fun time getting her ready together, and because of that, she already considered the date a huge success.

She turned to give her mom a quick hug before stuffing her arms through her coat. "Brenna will come by to get you for supper," she informed her. "She also said she's willing to play cards again with you but, seriously, try to let her win at least one game this time."

"I *tried* to let her win last time," her mom said with a roll of her eyes. "She's just *really* bad at cribbage." She made a shooing motion with her hands, laughing as she did. "Now get going and have fun."

This was the mother Kate had known all her life—the kind, fun-loving woman who had raised her with everything she had to offer. She loved it when these glimpses of sunshine reached through the clouds. Now these episodes of perfect lucidity and bliss were much fewer and far between.

Over the past few weeks, her mother had started forgetting more about their life together, and her short-term memory was whittled away more and more with each passing day. It wasn't just thoughts, either. She'd now moved into the territory of forgetting processes and skills, too. This all worried Kate terribly.

"Are you sure you'll be all right until Brenna gets here?" she asked, biting her lip. Maybe she should stay behind and enjoy her mother's good mood.

She shook her head vigorously and shoved Kate toward the door. "What am I? A kid? Get out of here. Go!"

Jack laughed. "Thanks for letting me borrow Kate for a few hours. I promise I'll have her home by curfew, Mrs. Griffin."

Her mother slapped his arm playfully, almost flirtatiously. "Oh, I'm sure you will, you smooth talker," she said while batting her eyelashes. "I just wish I'd had the chance to meet you first before you took my daughter out."

Kate's heart sunk. So much for lucidity. She cleared her throat, waiting to see what Jack would say to dispel the situation.

He took both of her mother's hands in his. "My name is Jack and we have met before, Nancy. You come to my office a few times per week to talk about things as part of your treatment, and you're one of my favorite patients."

Her mom gave him a puzzled look then slowly nodded. "Oh, right," she said in a way that told Kate she was still very much confused but just trying to save face in the awkward situation. "Well, just take care of my little girl, okay?"

Kate knew her mother was trying to set everyone's mind at ease but also that she must be quite distressed at having forgotten Jack's acquaintance.

She leaned in close to him and whispered, "I think I better stay here."

He put a hand on her shoulder and shook his head. "I

know you're worried, but there's nothing you can do right now. Brenna will be here soon. Everything will be fine," he assured her.

Kate glanced back toward her mother, a frown tugging down both corners of her mouth. "Mom, are you sure you don't want me to stay?"

"No!" she snapped, ripping her hands away from Jack. "I'm going to have a nap. I think I can manage that on my own, for goodness sake."

"I'll be home soon, Mom," she said, fighting back tears for all of their sakes.

Jack waited for her pass through the door before him.

She tried to push the feelings of guilt away as she walked beside him toward his car parked up at the main house. With the upcoming change of seasons, the sun now hung in the sky into the early evening hours, which meant they thankfully still had a bit of light by which to navigate the paths.

"I promise," Jack said, taking her hand in his and giving it a gently squeeze. "Everything's going to be all right. Try to relax and have some fun tonight, if you can."

She shrugged and kicked at the path. Would the intense guilt ever let up?

"Hey, stop scowling like that," Jack said, bumping her shoulder with his. "We don't want anyone thinking I'm holding you at gunpoint to get you to spend some time with me."

Kate couldn't resist the smile that blossomed on her face. Jack was right, of course. Even though she still hadn't learned their destination, he was taking her somewhere fun, not dragging her in front of a firing squad.

"You know," she said, noticing his hand hadn't yet let go of hers. "I could've driven in to town to meet you so that you wouldn't have to drive me back after."

Jack clucked his tongue. "That wouldn't be a very gentlemanly thing for me to do, now would it?"

The laugh that bubbled from her chest felt so freeing. Jack's hand emanated so much warmth it seemed to be sending the heat right through her whole body. Did he realize he was still holding her hand? Did he enjoy this simple touch as much as she did?

When they reached his car, Jack bowed and opened the door with a flourish.

Her cheeks had already begun to hurt from smiling so much over the past couple minutes, and they hadn't even left the ranch yet. It was amazing how quickly he had helped to lift her spirits. "I swear, if you tell me my chariot awaits or anything else even remotely corny like that, I'm turning around and running back to the safety of my cabin."

He brought his hand up to his chest, pretending she'd

mortally wounded him. "I wasn't going to do any such thing."

She slid onto the leather seat, and before Jack could close the door, he bent down and grinned at her. "Besides, it's not a chariot. It's a Honda."

CHAPTER 12

THE SIMPLE STRIP MALL HAD A QUIET, UNASSUMING FAÇADE, but as Jack and Kate entered the building, it was like they'd been transported to an indoor Renaissance fair. The smell of cooked meats and wood chips permeated the air.

"Should I have worn a costume or something?" Kate asked with a giggle, eyeing the colorful banners that festooned the large open space.

"Don't worry about it. We're actually headed downstairs," he assured her.

"Ooh, what's downstairs?"

Jack simply shook his head and gave her a sly wink as he led her through minstrels and jugglers and around a fighting pit where two knights in armor beat on each other with metal bars. The atmosphere was certainly lively, confusing, and exciting—and all at once, too.

Even as they descended the shield covered stairwell, the jovial atmosphere filled Kate with a nervous sense of wonder.

"You ready to throw some axes?" Jack asked with a sweeping gesture towards a surreal bowling alley of wooden stalls set up with racks that held a variety of axes and knives.

Groups of people stood around laughing as their party members attempted throws, sometimes clumsily and sometimes with expert precision.

"You want me to do what?" Kate widened her eyes. It was the only way she could take in the whole scene as Jack guided her right into the fray, pointing at a wooden target riddled with large welts.

"We're throwing axes. C'mon. Just line up here," he said, matching his actions to his words. "Grip the axe, raise it up and release!"

Kate watched as the axe tumbled end over end finishing with a loud *thunk!* as it hit the center of the wooden target. *Had he lost his mind?* Who brought a date to some place where you threw deadly weapons around?

She could see now that it was a good thing she hadn't worn anything dressier. If she'd tried doing this in a skirt, she was sure she'd have looked ridiculous—and possibly taken an eye out, too.

"This doesn't seem like the safest idea." She examined the lightweight axe in her hand, moving it from side to side to get a good look at it. It looked really sharp and not at all like something she should try to fling across the room.

"Here, put your legs like this, and just hold it up high enough that when you throw it you get a good, clean thrust." He stood beside her with his legs spread slightly apart, knees bent and holding his hands up in the air.

She tried unsuccessfully to hold her laughter in, but everything about the entire situation was so absurd. "You look like a caveman attacking a wooly mammoth."

He laughed and stood back up. "Okay, well, then why don't you show me how I should be doing it without looking ridiculous?"

She shook her head and shrugged. "I have no clue. This was your idea, remember?"

"Then trust me a little bit. The last thing I want to see happen is you throwing an axe into your foot. Or mine. *Ouch.*"

Her mouth dropped open in horror. "Are you serious?" The image of an axe stuck in her foot flashed through her mind in grisly detail.

"Now what kind of gentleman would I be if I let my date get disfigured?" He lifted his shoulders. "Besides, who knows if you can do it until you actually try throwing it?"

He came over and stood behind her, lifting her arms up in the air.

She could feel his breath on her neck as he helped her get

into the proper position. When he finally spoke, her entire body trembled from how close his body stood behind hers.

"Imagine a large horizontal plane extending in front of you from your waist. These axes are balanced to help you throw them, so just make sure to release before you cross the horizontal plane. The earlier your release, the higher it will go. The later, the lower. Okay, now throw it as hard as you can so it sticks in the target instead of bouncing off. This is your chance to let your frustrations out. Trust me, it feels so good."

Her heart was racing, but she wasn't sure if it was from the adrenaline for what she was about to do, or the fact that this man had her completely flustered. She really shouldn't be throwing an axe when she was feeling like this.

But then again, he had mentioned letting frustrations out and—oh—did Kate have plenty of those.

When he stepped back, she brought her hands back to wind up and throw, determined to give it her best shot. When the axe flew through the air and hit the wooden board at the end, she jumped up and down with excitement. It wasn't anywhere near the target, but she'd at least managed not to lop off any body parts.

She spun around and faced Jack with a huge grin on her face. "That was amazing!"

He was grinning almost as big as her as he handed her another axe and stepped back. "Good. Try again."

She took a deep breath, squared her shoulders, and hurled the axe through the air. With a *fwip* and a *thunk*, it embedded in the edge of the target. Clapping her hands, she laughed out loud at how good it felt.

Jack walked past her to go retrieve the axes from the wood. He glanced back at her in mock concern. "Could you hold off throwing more until I get back behind you?"

Kate tested the heft of the remaining axe. "Hmmm. I don't know." She laughed when he pretended to cower.

As he stepped up next to her, he handed her back an axe. "Okay, so what do you say we make this interesting?"

"What more interesting that hurling deadly weapons of Medieval warfare around?"

Jack chuckled. "Yeah, how about a quick game to twenty-one? Outer ring is one, inner ring is three, and bullseye is five."

"What are the stakes?" The tension in the air suddenly seemed to shift, and she realized with a start that she'd been flirting shamelessly with him almost from the very moment they'd walked out the door of her cabin. It was a side of her she'd never known before.

And he'd been right. She was having so much fun.

"Oh, it's pretty high stakes." He pretended to think this over before widening his eyes. "If I win, I get a kiss."

Her breathing slowed and everything around them seemed to grow quiet. She could vaguely hear axes being thrown in the sections on either side of them, and people cheering, but right now, she was being held in the gaze of this man in front of her.

"And what if I win?" Her mouth was suddenly dry.

He caught her eye and sent her an exaggerated wink. "Well, that's up to you."

She swallowed and tried to keep her breathing even. "I'll have to think about what I want when I win, then," she said with a wink back. Winning would be great fun, but it seemed losing might be just as nice.

Carefully, she took aim and contemplated throwing it to the side and not even trying to win. But she didn't want to be too obvious, and her competitive nature wasn't going to let her just give up that easily.

A flurry of axes made their way down the range into wooden targets, each hit accompanied by a shout of triumph or flirtatious joke. As the score slowly climbed, Kate felt like a rubber band untwisting, tightness leaving her body. Each axe left her hands with complete abandon, taking with it all of her pent-up anger over the unfairness of life. At the same time, it had become more than a game, almost a type of therapy. But as the tension released, nervous excitement built, too. Soon one of them would hit twenty-one points, and then...

She swallowed just thinking about the prospect of this small intimacy with Jack. She'd daydreamed about it for so long, but now that it was a true possibility, she didn't know what to wish for.

"Okay," Jack announced with a smirk. "That brings the score up to twenty and sixteen. Your turn, oh, and do you want some ChapStick?"

"Don't get cocky now," she teased.

With a fluid motion, she raised the axe high and let it fly. It tipped end over end twice before smacking right into the bullseye.

"Ha!" she yelled triumphantly. "That makes twenty-one. I win."

Kate did a little jump but landed on shaky feet. Her entire body suddenly seemed too weak to hold her up, as though every emotion she'd been holding in for so long was all that had been keeping her going.

She shivered and looked over at Jack, who put a concerned arm around Kate's waist to steady her. "Are you okay?" he asked, lines creasing his face.

She nodded weakly as she tried to get her emotions back under control. Jack pulled her closer in a kind of supportive hug, letting her use him to keep from becoming a puddle on the ground.

His fingers stroked through her hair as she rested her head on his shoulder. "I think you needed to do this. I had a feeling it would be good for you. It's good for me, too. I've been coming here ever since the place went up. We all have frustrations to work out, and it's better to throw an axe at a target then to take it out on another human being."

Kate felt silly having him hold her like this. She didn't know what had come over her, but for the first time in longer than she could remember, the ball of tension she carried everywhere unknotted and slipped away. Now her body didn't know how to react to its sudden absence.

When she finally thought she had the strength to hold herself on her own, she pulled back, reluctant to let go. He smiled at her, taking away any embarrassment she was feeling.

"You won, fair and square, and I always pay up on my wagers. Just remember, I'm not a wealthy man in case you were—"

She took a deep breath and grabbed the front of Jack's shirt. "Shut up and kiss me."

As soon as the words came out of her mouth, she had to fight herself not to turn away and take them back. She had never been the type of woman to be so forward with a man. But then his lips met hers, and then her doubts, problems, embarrassment, everything just melted away.

This was more than a school-girl crush, and as the lightning rushed through her body from their kiss, she knew just how serious it had already become. Right now, her heart wasn't just beating wildly in her chest. It was already falling hopelessly in love.

CHAPTER 13

THE STREETLIGHTS WASHED OVER THE CAR IN A HYPNOTIC pattern, lulling Kate into a near sleep though she was giddy with happiness following the amazing night she and Jack had shared. He held onto her hand tightly as he drove them both back to the ranch, neither of them wanting to break the connection this gesture brought.

After the axe throwing, they'd gone back upstairs to partake in the odd cuisine being served in the main Renaissance area. Once their bellies were comfortably full, they strolled hand-in-hand through downtown Anchorage. It was a fun walk during which they talked about the unique and shared experiences growing up in Alaska. The streets were almost deserted, so the sounds of their laughter would occasionally echo off the buildings.

Jack, for his part, had proven to be a man of many faces.

She'd seen his serious side when working with his patients, and his caring side when he'd helped to nurture Hope through the night. But on this night, he'd put on the best face of them all. He'd been teasing and fun with the axe throwing, tender and attentive during their kiss. He read each moment perfectly, and Kate fell harder and harder for him with each additional moment spent in his company.

That was the thing about Doctor Jack Young...he wasn't boring.

"I still can't believe you came up with axe throwing as the plan for our first date," she teased as he started up the car to drive them back to the ranch.

He scoffed and briefly looked over at her, the lights of a passing car illuminating his face. "You had fun, didn't you?"

She laughed. "I did. But now I'm kind of wondering about you and Renaissance fairs. Is this a regular thing for you?" Kate gasped in mock horror. "Do you have a costume? Do you dress up on the weekends to play knight and vassal?"

They both laughed like silly children.

"No, it's nothing like that. I just wanted to take you somewhere fun. You're always so stuck in the here and now. I thought you could use a little play."

"And axe throwing is the first thing that springs to mind when you think 'play?' Do you take all your dates there?" She couldn't stop laughing, but luckily Jack matched her fits of laughter equally with his own.

"For your information, I don't date all that much, so there is no 'all my dates' to consider. *All my dates* is you, Kate, and—yes—I've thought long and hard about where I would take you for a date if I ever got the chance."

"Hmmm, interesting," she said in an accent she thought sounded like one of those famous therapists. She turned toward him in her seat and brought one hand to her chin while still hanging tight to his hand with her other. "And how long have you been planning *zis* date?"

He shook his head and blew out a long gust of air. "You remember your first day on the ranch?"

His response surprised her so, that she dropped the fake accent. "What? That soon?"

"No, don't be ridiculous." He glanced at her briefly before turning back to the road. "It was the next day."

So the whole time she'd been crushing on Jack he'd been carrying a torch for her as well? *Unbelievable.*

"So you liked it, then?" he asked, sliding his hands up and down the steering wheel nervously.

"Oh, yes. It was actually kind of perfect," she assured him. "Who would have ever thought throwing an axe could be so therapeutic?"

"Me. I did," he said with a relieved chuckle. "I've always done stuff like that whenever I felt like the world starting to weigh me down. I used to do a lot of boxing. And karate. When they opened up the Ren fair, I thought it would be another fun way to work through any pent-up frustrations."

She thought about this for a moment. "I get what you're saying. I do. I just can't picture you as the kind of man who would need to vent out frustrations."

He didn't say anything for a few seconds, then shrugged. "Early on it was only about dealing with the anger of people mistreating my brother. That and the injustice of the hand he was dealt. As I got older and started training as a thera-pist, I found myself taking more and more of my work home with me. After a while, it just builds up until you feel trapped beneath the debris of other people's misfortunes."

She let out a slow breath. "Wow. I guess I never thought about what it's like on the other side of the therapy."

"Most people don't," he said, squeezing her hand again. "But almost as soon as I met you, I recognized you had that same buildup of tension in you that I always used to carry around me, too. Some people call it the savior complex. I call it being a good person."

"Yeah, I didn't even realize how much I needed to do something like that. And the meal was perfect, too. Thank you." She smiled at him and waited for him to look over at her. As she let her eyes move over the outline of his face in the dark car, her heart did a little flutter. When he finally did turn to meet her eyes, her breath caught in her throat again.

Would she ever be able to act normal around this man?

How could a simple look from him cause her normal bodily functions to go haywire?

"It was my pleasure," he said with an enormous, sincere grin. "How about next time we hit up the shooting range? Or should we skip right to the heavy explosives?"

Kate laughed noncommittally. They would be at the ranch in just a few minutes, and she was already on edge anticipating another kiss. After the first one they'd shared, she wasn't sure it could be topped, but she was definitely willing to reserve that particular judgment.

"Are you sure this isn't improper?" she asked as her old worries began to resurface once more. "For us to be seeing each other like this?"

She didn't know why she couldn't let it go, but she still had a niggling worry that maybe she was getting in over her head with someone she shouldn't be. Otherwise, things just seemed too perfect. Maybe it was the fact they were almost back to their daily lives that brought the differences they'd experienced tonight into such stark contrast.

"It's a gray area for sure. I mean, you're not my patient. And I won't be your mother's therapist long-term. If she starts to decline more rapidly, therapy could actually hurt rather than help. Her sense of the world around her will change once again and, well, I won't be needed anymore."

His eyes searched for hers again in the darkness. "But that's when I hope you will let me be there for you. Not as a therapist—as someone who cares about you and who wants to help you through what I know is ahead. And if you're worried about the propriety of things, I can ask for one of my colleagues to come out and take over her case."

Kate looked out the window into the darkness. It wasn't like she hadn't known therapy would be a temporary thing for her mother. Already the progress she'd seen since moving to the ranch had taken a sharp turn. She was having more bad days than good now. It was only a matter of time.

Once the disease stole her memory completely, there wouldn't be anything Jack could do to help her. Kate just hoped that she'd still be able to make a difference when that time came—because it was coming up on them awfully fast.

Guilt rose up in her chest again as she realized she'd barely even thought about her mother during their date that night. It was like she was already gone, and Kate had gone out to have fun without a care in the world.

She wished she could do that, but her reality was tied up in what was happening with her mom. There was no avoiding that.

Jack squeezed her hand. "I'm glad we were able to get away from the ranch for a while. And I want you to know that you don't need to go through any of this alone. I'm here and will do whatever I can to help." Was he saying this as a therapist who specialized in memory disorders or was he perhaps offering more?

Kate wanted to ask him, but before she could, her phone beeped to tell inform her of a new text message. When she pulled out her phone and glanced down at the screen, she saw Brenna's name and number illuminated. A growing sense of doom descended upon her as she clicked to read the message. Make that series of messages. More were coming in as she read.

Kate, I'm so sorry!

I helped your mom get ready for bed after our game.

She said she was tired.

When I left she was already sleeping.

But she must have got up at some time after that.

Kate waited for Brenna to type out her next message. She didn't like where this was going, and she needed to know now. Was her mother safe? Or…?

Another message popped up: *I went back to check on her an hour later…*

Oh no, oh no, oh no. Kate already knew what was coming next. Sure enough Brenna's next message revealed: *And she was gone.*

Kate's heart sunk to her feet and the world around her started to spin. She cried aloud and shoved the phone at Jack.

"What's wrong?" he asked. When she didn't answer, unable to form the words she needed, he squeezed her hand again. "Kate, what happened? Do I need to pull over?"

"My mom is missing," she finally managed to cry. "She's out in the cold somewhere. They can't find her."

Jack wrapped both hands even tighter on the wheel as he pushed down on the accelerator.

But it was all for naught.

Kate knew they wouldn't get there fast enough.

She should never have left her mom alone.

This was all her fault.

CHAPTER 14

Jack could barely pull his car to a stop before Kate flung the door wide open and raced across the yard toward her cabin.

As soon as she reached the steps, Brenna barreled out the door and wrapped Kate in a tight hug. Her entire body shook as she clung to her friend. "I'm sorry. I'm so, so sorry. I should have stayed with her, but she was in bed and asleep, so I thought she'd be okay. We've looked all around the cabins but can't find her anywhere."

Brenna heaved giant sobs as she pulled back to search Kate's eyes. Her cheeks were chapped red from the cold and patchy from the huge streams of tears that continued to fall freely.

Kate shook her head and put a hand on Brenna's arm to steady her. "It's not your fault. I should have been here."

"Kate, no. Don't do that to yourself." Jack's voice reached her ears as he tugged on her arm and forced her to look at him. "You can't blame yourself. This is an unfortunate circumstance that happened because of her disease. It's not something you can put on yourself or anyone else."

Her boss, Elizabeth Jane, appeared from between the cabins, shaking her head in sorrow. "Jack's right. Dorian and some of the ranch hands have split up on horseback to check the trails and woods, and the others are on foot going through some of the deeper brush. I would tell you to just stay here until we find her, but I know there's no use, so I told Howard to get a couple more horses saddled for you and Jack to join the search."

Kate didn't hesitate. She spun on her heel, which almost threw her into the snow as she raced to the barn, ignoring the normal paths in the snow. The shortest distance was a straight line, so she cut a beeline right for the horses. Buddy was already saddled, so she swung herself up on him and spurred him out into the cold night.

She pushed blindly down the path Buddy chose, her eyes had already nearly frozen shut from the unforgiving combination of her tears and the cold night.

"Kate, slow down!" someone called form behind her.

But she refused to listen as she leaned closer to Buddy's neck and urged him to go faster still. The other rider matched her accelerated pace until the quick clopping steps were right upon her.

"Whoa, there!" Jack shouted to Buddy as he grabbed the reins from Kate.

"Let me go. I have to find my mom!" Kate yelled at him, her voice breaking apart in tears.

"No way," he said, slowing both of their steeds to a gentle walk. "Your eyes are practically iced over. Can you even see? You could race right by her and not notice."

"She could be anywhere by now. I have to find her. Let go of me."

"No. Kate, stop. Look at me." His voice was firm and inflexible. He'd never spoken to her like this before. "You need to think about where you're even going to search. She can't be that far. Brenna was only gone for an hour between the time your mom went to sleep and the time she found her missing. At the most, she's only been out for about an hour and a half by now. She's close by. Can't you feel it?"

She blinked hard while listening to him. Each flutter of her eyelashes melted more of the ice that had begun to collect around her tear-soaked eyes. Jack's words made sense but did little to quell the panic and adrenaline that surged through her veins. If only she could keep racing through the open field and away from everything, back in time, back to before the illness had robbed her of a mother.

But, no—as much as she wanted it, there was no going back. Only forward.

Defeated, she guided Buddy to a stop, her breathing as heavy as the horse's beneath her. Suddenly she couldn't hold it together anymore, and a sob tore from her throat. "Jack, I shouldn't have left her alone. I know you're going to say it wasn't my fault, but it was. It is. She needed me, and I wasn't here."

Jack backed his horse up until it stood beside Buddy once again. He placed a calming hand on her leg, but it wasn't enough to stop her crying. Only finding her mother would be enough.

"Kate, we're going to find her," he said. "Please, don't do this to yourself. You can't blame yourself for your mother's illness or what happens because of it. This is not your fault. Do you understand me?" His firm gaze brooked no argument, but Kate couldn't see any version of events where the blame didn't rest squarely on her own shoulders.

"But if I had been here…"

He seemed almost angry at her now. "You don't know that it would have been any different. If you'd gone out to check on Hope because your mom was sleeping and she got lost then, would you give up on Hope? If this happens when you're asleep, are you going to give up on sleep?"

"It's just that I'm her—"

"You're her daughter, I know, but that still doesn't mean this is your fault. Let's just focus on finding her, okay?"

He waited until Kate nodded her consent.

"Okay, great. Is there anywhere around here she seemed to like going to when you went for walks? Anything that might remind her of something from her distant past? Her short-term memory might be struggling, but she still remembers things that happened a long time ago as if they are fresh and new."

Kate tried to think, but her mind was just spinning in circles. She knew she had to pull herself together, but everything seemed to be falling apart right in front of them.

Finally, Jack's fingers reached up and wiped the fresh tears from her cheeks before cupping her face in his palm. "I promise. We'll find her."

He turned his horse back toward the ranch and urged Kate to do the same. "She couldn't have gone this far, even at a run. Let's go closer to the cabins. I bet we'll find her there."

Kate allowed him to guide her home as she moved her eyes across the landscape, closely examining every tree, bit of brush, and mound of snow they came across.

If we could just find her footprints in the snow...

They made their way down the twisting paths in darkness, the sound of the snow crunching under the horse's hooves with every step. Kate had been in such a hurry she hadn't even thought to grab a flashlight to aid in the search.

They both held onto their mounts with one hand and their phones with the other, using the tiny in-built flashlights to guide the way. The illumination didn't spread far, and it drained their batteries quickly.

Hopefully they'd have enough time to...

No, she couldn't think like that. She couldn't think about anything but finding her mother now.

They would find her. They had to. As far as Kate knew, every single person who worked on the ranch, and even a lot of the guests who'd heard about it, were out in the frigid night to assist in the search.

When they turned back their horses to go down the same trail a third time, Kate felt the hope dying within her. "What if we can't find her in time?" she cried to Jack beside her. "It's already been a couple hours. She's got to be so cold by now."

Her voice shook with emotion as she caught up to Jack. He'd stopped and turned to face her. The moon was bright in the sky, giving off enough light that she was able to discern the determined set of his jaw. He wasn't planning on giving up. No, there was something comforting in his eyes that told her he wouldn't rest until they found her.

"You don't know that," he reminded her. "She might be somewhere warm. She could be totally safe and having a good time for all we know."

His hand reached out for hers, and she let him take it.

"Are you sure you can't think of where she might have gone? Sometimes people with memory issues will go to a place they associate with something from their past. What's nearby that might be meaningful to her?"

Kate thought hard about this, searching every conversation, every memory, until at last she had something. "When we went for a walk the first week she was here we found a group of bushes behind the main house that she said looked like a fort she'd had when she was a little girl. She even crawled right into the middle of them and made me get in with her. Of course! Why didn't I think of that before?"

How had she been so stupid? Jack had already asked her to scour her mind for possibilities, but she'd been so focused on her anxiety that she hadn't managed to remember those bushes until now.

"Show me." Jack waited for her to take the lead as they made their way back to the yard.

"It was kind of off the path a bit," she explained, pressing her heels into Buddy's sides so he would quicken the pace. "Mom said she didn't like staying on the path because you only got to see the same things everyone else did."

She led the past the house and kept following the path until she found the spot she remembered from that day. It had been such a good day, so carefree. They retraced those steps carefully, Kate struggling to recall each turn they'd taken, each twist through the open field. Then, as she strained her eyes against the wind, something miraculous happened.

"I see tracks!" she cried, nudging Buddy to go faster until they came upon the copse of bushes her mother had imagined as a fort so many weeks ago.

"Jack!" she cried again, pointing toward the brush with a shaking finger. She was so happy and so terrified, all at the same time. Would her mother be waiting within the warmth of those branches? Was everything okay now?

"Stay here," he instructed. "I'll go in and get her." Jack was already off his horse and pushing past her as she dismounted, too. But before she could even reach the edge of the brush, Jack was already on his way back out.

And in his arms he held the limp body of her mother.

CHAPTER 15

Machines whirred and beeped in a macabre dirge as Kate leaned forward to rest her arms on the rails of her mother's hospital bed. She couldn't tear her eyes away as her mother's chest rose and fell with every shallow breath. Each new intake of air brought her more and more comfort, but also reminded her of how close she'd come to losing the one person who mattered most.

She refused to leave her mother's side—not for sleep, food, or anything else. Ever since Jack had emerged from the brush with her lifeless body is his arms, she'd been unable to pull herself away.

First, they'd ridden like the wind back to the house, and then she'd stood by helpless while Jack performed CPR. She felt almost completely numb by the time the ambulance arrived to transport them to the hospital. The paramedics had even questioned whether there might be something wrong with her as well. At the hospital, Kate ambled through the halls like a zombie as she trailed after her mother's gurney.

Now, as the first rays of light started to peek through the slats in the blinds, the numbness finally fell away, and the pain reverberated through her with shocking intensity. Kate's head dropped into her hands as she recalled the terror that had overtaken her during their search for her missing mother. She cried, too, for the other worries she'd harbored over the past few months, cried because she could no longer pretend that her mother might one day get better.

True, she would recover from being out in the cold tonight, but that wasn't the problem. Last night had offered indisputable proof that the disease couldn't be stopped, that it was taking over, and soon Kate would be an orphan.

As her mother continued to sleep beside her, Kate silently swiped at her tears.

Already, she felt so alone.

Jack reentered the room, reminding her that she didn't have to go through this alone. He'd stayed by her side while they got her mom settled and only left to secure coffee or snacks, which is what he'd brought for Kate now. He'd also helped to guide her through what would likely happen next with her mother's care and how to best handle it as her primary caregiver. Though it all, he'd become a stable presence in the storm that had taken over her life.

And she didn't deserve it one bit.

He placed the steaming cups of coffee on a side table, then pulled her up and into his arms. He just held her and let her cry while the machines beeped around them.

"Sorry," she said, failing to hide the tremor in her voice. "It's been a bit of a rollercoaster since last night."

Jack brushed a piece of her hair back and tucked it behind her ear. "I think for you it's been more than just that. You had a lot of tears you needed to get out."

She laughed nervously, not wanting to look into his kind face. "I think my tear ducts have run dry."

He brought up his other hand to wipe some of the wetness from her cheek. "Honestly, I don't know how you've been holding it together this long. You have no siblings or family to help you, so you've been trying to do it all alone. It's too much for one person to deal with. Please tell me you know that now."

She sighed and pulled herself from his embrace. "I don't have any choice," she said, shifting her gaze to the floor as she shook her head emphatically. "There isn't anyone else to do it."

"There is now. Let me help you get through this." He tried to take her hand, but she crossed her arms over her chest.

Kate lifted her eyes to his and swallowed hard. He looked sincere, but everything in her life was such a jumble right now. The last thing she needed was a man who wanted to be there for the long haul now, but then changed his mind later as things got harder and harder. What she needed to focus on now was her mom—not the possibility of a new relationship.

No matter how much she'd let herself want it before.

It shouldn't take him too long to get over plain Kate when any woman would be lucky to have Jack's attentions. She hated to let him down, but he'd survive it. Letting down her mother could cost her so much more.

She took a couple steps back and leaned against the wall. "I'm sorry, Jack. I really like you, but this thing between us just isn't going to work. I need to be fully present to help Mom in whatever way she needs it. I don't have time to try to fit you into the picture, too."

Jack's gaze floated toward her mother before he turned back to Kate with a deep frown. "Well, you already know how I feel. You need to learn to accept help from other people and not expect everything to come with impossibly tangled strings attached. I like you, you like me. It doesn't have to be any more complicated than that. I'm not asking you to commit your life to me. Only for you to give me a chance. When and if you need me, I'll be here for you. Not just for this, but for anything."

She nodded but didn't know what else she could say. She just didn't have the strength to take this conversation any further, and Jack seemed to know that.

He turned his back to her, and for a moment she thought he'd leave then and there. Instead, he grabbed one of the Styrofoam coffee cups and extended in out to her. "Here," he said. "You look like you could use this."

Kate accepted it gratefully, taking a seat in the nearby armchair and watching her mom again as she took a sip. The warm liquid left a trail down her throat, and she closed her eyes to savor the taste. "Thank you. How did you know I liked French Vanilla creamer?"

He laughed softly as he pulled up a chair beside her, taking the other coffee cup for himself. "You had your own bottle in the fridge, remember? I've never seen anyone put so much in one cup of coffee before."

Closing her eyes again, she smiled to herself as she remembered the night they'd spent nursing Hope. It seemed like a lifetime ago already with everything that had happened since then.

Jack cleared his throat. "I have a list of places that specialize in caring for Alzheimer's patients. If you want, I can call around and see what's available."

She blinked her eyes open, looking toward him in confusion. He knew that this wasn't what she wanted, so why was he pushing it yet again?

Before she could say anything, he raised his hand to stop her. "Kate, you know it's time. You can't be with her twenty-four hours a day. She needs to be somewhere safe. Please do this for her. Do it for yourself, too."

Her eyes fell to look at the cup gripped tightly between her hands. A tear fell and splattered on the plastic lid below. "I want her to be safe, but I just don't know if I'm ready to sign her life away to someone else."

"You're not signing her life away. This isn't your fault. It never has been. You're making the best and most informed decision for her care. It doesn't mean you'll stop loving her. Sometimes loving someone means doing things that might cause them or us pain. This is one of those times, Kate."

She wished she could yell and scream at Jack, tell him he had it all wrong.

But she couldn't hide from the truth anymore. Last night had made sure of that.

It was time.

CHAPTER 16

KATE SCRATCHED BEHIND HOPE'S EARS AS THE HORSE PRESSED its spindly body into hers. While Kate's mother was steadily declining, Hope had been improving by leaps and bounds each day, providing a stark contrast in Kate's world.

Her world and work at the ranch had taken on a whole new level of difficulty these past few days. Thankfully, the hospital had agreed to keep her mother in their long-term care wing until Kate could secure a more permanent arrangement. She'd finally admitted that her mother needed full-time care and a secure facility. The ranch had been wonderful, but it was no longer enough.

In just the past week, Kate's mom had deteriorated so much that it nearly broke her in two. She'd know it was coming, but seeing it firsthand was a different kind of awful. Kate had done her research, read about Alzheimer's stories, thought she'd known what she would be up against. But living the reality was so much worse than any eventuality she'd been able to imagine.

To look her own mother in the eye and have her not fully recognize who she was seeing... Absolutely heartbreaking.

Thankfully, Kate's mother still seemed to know her, even if the recollection came back to her slowly or required a gentle nudge. They'd reached this point so quickly, it wouldn't be long before they reached the next, the point where Kate's mother didn't remember her even with help. As for now, Kate's heart broke all over again whenever she had to remind her mother of their relationship.

Jack volunteered to do most of the heavy lifting when it came to researching and visiting assisted living facilities. He had found a few good candidates to consider. He'd really proven to be a lifesaver in planning the next stage of her mother's care, but Kate knew in her heart that she wasn't being fair to him about their situation. Outside of conversations about her mother, she'd avoided the kindly therapist as much as she possibly could. Being in his company reminded her of just how much she was letting go. Besides, she could never look at Jack now without recalling that terrible night.

They were finished before they'd even gotten the chance to fully get started—and that was just the way it had to be. As much as she loved working with the horses on the ranch, she might need to find another job and move on from there as well.

At least she'd managed to save Hope during her brief tenure at Memory Ranch.

The vet had come to examine her again that day, and Kate was expecting good news.

Sure enough, the vet finished looking Hope over, then rose to his full height and addressed Kate with a giant grin on his face. "Well, I'll be," he said. "It's almost as if she's a completely different animal now. You've performed a miracle here. To be honest, I really didn't think she was going to make it, but it seems this little filly was just bound and determined to prove me wrong."

He patted Hope on the flank and chuckled before stooping down again to pack up his equipment.

Kate's breath hitched in her chest. She'd expected this news but still found it overwhelming to hear aloud. "So, she's fine?" she asked, chancing a smile of her own.

"Clean bill of health. All that's left now is just the growing." He finished preparing his bag then clapped a hand on her shoulder. "Keep up the good work."

She walked with him to the edge of the pen and waved goodbye before returning to Hope's side. The precious little horse rested her head on Kate's shoulder and leaned into her. Her body was still underweight, and she'd need to grow into her extra-long legs but still come out on the other side.

This was the other side.

At least Kate had managed to save someone.

The little foal had formed something of a maternal bond with Kate, trusting her above anyone else. She was still skittish around most other people, though, including all of the ranch hands who'd helped her along the way. The only other person she seemed to trust fully was Jack. It really was too bad she'd soon have to say goodbye to them both.

Kate's heart clenched just thinking about it. She would be the first to admit that she had let her feelings for him become too strong during their brief friendship, but that didn't lessen her resolve one bit. Their hearts may have matched, but the timing just didn't work. This was the harsh reality of what her life had become, and she simply had to make choices that her heart didn't want.

"Hey." Jack's voice startled Kate. "I hope we aren't interrupting."

As much as she wished she could tell him this was a bad time for a visit, Hope's reaction made Kate hold her tongue.

Hope turned on hoof so fast, she almost fell down into the straw. That didn't stop her, though. She raced to the edge of her stall quicker than her uncoordinated body was able to carry her, but still managed to make it over in one piece.

Jack beamed at her from over the top of the wooden slats. "Hey, my girl! Look at you running around like a big horse! Getting ready for the Kentucky Derby, are you? Well, don't tell the others, but I'm definitely placing my money on you."

He laughed as he opened the stall door and leaned down to pat Hope on her oversized head. She lapped up every second with Jack. The moment he moved the rest of the way into the stall, the little horse began hopping around to show off how much better she could move now.

Kate stood back and crossed her arms over her chest, her heart swelling as she watched the filly and man play.

"It's okay," Jack shouted behind him. "You can come in."

Another man several inches shorter than Jack but with his same dark coloring, shuffled into the stall, kicking the hay as he approached.

Jack put an arm over the newcomer's shoulders and turned him toward Kate with a huge smile splashed across his face. "I was hoping you'd be around because I have someone very special to introduce you to."

The stranger before her could only be Jack's beloved brother. He beamed at her, shoving his hand forward in greeting. "Hello!" he cried.

Jack made the official introduction. "This is my brother, Marty. Marty, this is Kate."

She smiled warmly at his brother. "I'm so happy to meet you, Marty. I hear you're pretty good with horses." She shook his outstretched hand and gave it a good squeeze.

"Yes, I am," he answered proudly.

"Well then," Jack said with a funny tilt of his head. "Meet Hope. She's the little foal I was telling you about."

Hope hesitated, not sure what to think of the new person. She twitched her tail nervously as Marty took careful steps forward.

"Hi, Hope. You can come over. I won't hurt you." As soon as Marty spoke, the horse set her head forward and closed the gap between them.

Kate's mouth dropped open in surprise as she watched how quickly Marty earned Hope's trust. Her eyes met Jack's in question, but he just shrugged.

"I told you he was good with horses," he said with an ever-widening grin.

"She's a nice horse," Marty said, petting Hope's neck. "I'm glad you saved her."

Kate laughed softly. "Well, she did the hard work. We just tried to help her along the way." She basked in Marty's praise. Even though so many others had told her the same, somehow his compliments felt even more sincere.

"We should take her outside so she can see the sun. It's so nice out today." Marty started walking out of the pen with Hope right behind him.

Jack went over and stopped him by placing a hand on his shoulder. "Marty, that's something that Kate needs to decide.

Remember, Hope isn't as strong as the other horses here, so we have to be extra careful with her."

Marty glanced toward Kate, awaiting her decree.

"Well, I was actually going to take her out for a bit today, so..." She smiled and nodded her encouragement, making Marty's face light up with joy. "Let's do it. I'm glad you came along to help me."

The three of them strode toward the exit, and as soon as she pushed the big door open, Hope raced outside as fast as her spindly legs could carry her. Thankfully, Kate had already moved all of the other horses from the pen on the other side of the door so Hope could explore the outside without any trouble.

Eventually she'd get the chance to meet the other horses, but she needed more time to grow and get stronger first. When the time came, Kate hoped they could find at least one who would spend the time to teach Hope proper "horse manners." Growing up with just human contact was never good for a horse, and she suspected Buddy would readily take the new herd member under his wing.

Marty patiently walked alongside Hope, watching with glee as she sniffed and kicked and jumped around the small penned-in area. Anchorage's famous breakup season had arrived, meaning the ground was covered with slush and mud as a result of the melting snow drifts.

Kate cringed as she watched Hope slip about in the mud

but kept reminding herself that it was good for the young horse to finally get to enjoy some fresh air. Simply put, this was something she hadn't believed possible even just one week ago.

"She looks happy to be outside," Jack said, coming over to stand next to her. "And she sure seems to have taken a liking to Marty. Thanks for letting him be a part of this."

She kept her eyes on Marty and Hope in an effort to ignore what Jack's nearness was doing to her heart. "Well, I knew it was time to let her have a taste of the outdoors. She's been cooped up in that barn since the day she was born. Nobody should have to live like that."

They stood together in companionable silence and watched as Hope became more and more confident with her new surroundings. Soon the young filly was running around the pen with complete abandon and only the occasional slip.

Kate smiled as she witnessed this new life enjoying everything around her with pure joy. To her eyes, Hope didn't have a care in the world and seemed to have already forgotten how hard she'd had to fight to stay alive just a few days ago.

But then Jack had to go and say something that brought reality crashing back upon them. "You've been avoiding me this week, Kate. Would you mind letting me know what I've done to upset you?"

Part of her wanted to just come clean and admit why

they couldn't be together, but she also knew he had a way of explaining things that could very well change her mind—and that was something she couldn't do.

Kate forced herself to be casual and said, "I've seen you up at the house a couple of times and I've talked to you a lot about the different facility options for my mom. I'd hardly say that's avoiding you."

Jack crossed his arms over his chest. "Yes, we do talk about that," he admitted. "But any other time I text or try to call and ask how you're doing, see if you'd maybe like to get together, you brush me off just as fast as you can. What am I supposed to make of that, Kate? Tell me, because I'd really like to know."

"I did," she said with a sigh. "I already told you that, right now, I need to focus on my mom. I don't have time for anything—or anyone—else." Her heart screamed out in pain even though her brain knew this was right. This was how things had to be.

Jack's fingers brushed against hers as he studied her with sparkling brown eyes. "Kate, I know you're going through a terrible time right now, and I promise, all I want is to just be there for you. You need someone in your corner. I know what's happening with your mom is tough, but it's worse alone. Don't shut me out."

Thankfully, Marty came over to them making sweeping gestures with his arms as he shouted, "Hope seems so happy now. She likes it outside."

Jack took a step away from Kate, and it made her feel so cold, so empty.

She forced a smile for Marty's benefit, but even he knew something was off.

"She does like it," Kate said, hoping to move past the topic of her and Jack once and for all. "Man, I don't know if she'll agree to come back in the barn now, but our little girl does need her rest."

She tried to laugh, but her eyes caught Jack's as she turned to walk beside Marty back in the direction of the exhausted little horse.

Disappointment and hurt clouded Jack's gaze, but he said nothing to stop them.

She wished she didn't have to hurt him, though obviously it was too late to change that. Kate liked him so much, but that didn't change the obstacles in their path.

Kate had been running hard and for a long time. She had no more strength left to jump the hurdles they'd need to clear to make things work between them.

Jack would just have to accept that. They were out of other options.

CHAPTER 17

A MILD BREEZE SHOOK THE NEWLY SPROUTED BUDS THAT HAD just started to peek out from the trees lining the ranch. Already the air was warmer than expected, considering the slush that still clung stubbornly to the ground. Kate loved this time of year because it meant warmer weather would soon be on its way.

She sat on her tiny cabin porch beside Brenna as the two discussed wedding plans over hot cocoa. No doubt Jack would be inside the big house working with his patients, so close to where she sat though it felt like miles away. At last he had gotten the message, and since the day in the pen with Hope and Marty, he'd mostly stopped trying to get in touch with her.

In fact, he'd only texted a few times here and there when he'd either heard from a facility about how long their waiting list was, or to tell Kate when he was headed to the hospital to visit her mother. Each communication became increasingly short and to the point, and Kate was grateful for it.

He was still conducting therapy sessions with her mother to help prepare her for the move to long-term care, but neither of them asked Kate to join anymore.

In just the past couple of weeks in the hospital, the disease had progressed rapidly. Kate suspected this was in part due to the fact her mother had just stopped fighting. Knowing that she'd lost her independence for good and that there would be no going back had finally defeated her strong spirit. Occasionally she'd still have a few angry outbursts, but even those were becoming fewer and farther between.

So far Kate had hung on at the ranch while searching for new career opportunities elsewhere. She didn't want to settle on anything until she knew where her mother would wind up so that she could ensure she'd always be just a quick drive away. It felt dishonest to keep working without disclosing her plans to leave, but she also suspected Elizabeth Jane knew it was only a matter of time. After all, she'd expressly taken the job here as a way of staying close to her mother. Now that her mother was moving on, she needed to, too.

How she'd miss the friends she'd made—Hope and Liz and Brenna, but most of all Jack.

"So it will just be you and my sister standing up with me. And of course Bigfoot will be performing a ribbon dance down the aisles to the tune of *Uptown Funk*," Brenna said, finally breaking through to Kate.

She shook her head as she tried to catch up on the conversation she'd only been partially present for. What else had she missed? "Huh? Bigfoot?"

"Oh, there you are," Brenna said with a smirk. "I was saying that the bouquets are going to be simple wildflowers and nothing fancy. I seriously just want everything to be casual and relaxing, so it won't be a huge wedding—just a few friends and family, and people from the ranch who really are like family anyway. How long has your mind been elsewhere?"

"I'm sorry." Kate sighed heavily. "I just have a lot on my mind these days, but I promise I'll be ready for everything on your big day."

Brenna chuckled, her wavy blonde hair blowing softly in the breeze. "You've spent the past fifteen minutes looking over toward the pen where Hope is outside with Howard, then back up to the main house where I watched Jack's car pull in. I'm pretty sure I could have got up and walked away when he stepped out of his car and went into the house without you even noticing. Why don't you just go up there and talk to him?"

"What? No way." Kate took a long, slow gulp of her cocoa, refusing to meet Brenna's eyes.

But Brenna pulled the mug away from her and forced Kate to give her full attention. "I can see the way you two look at each other. Even before you guys went on your date, you two very obviously have it bad for each other. Everyone here knows it. Why are you avoiding him when he's kind of exactly what you need right now?"

Kate groaned. "Are you really going to call me out on this right now?"

"Yup." Brenna smiled and relaxed back into her chair. "Now spill."

"What's there to tell? I like him, and I think he likes me, too. But the timing isn't right, which means nothing can come of it even if I wanted it to."

Brenna let out a quiet laugh. "You *think* he likes you? Kate, wow."

"What?" She crossed her arms over her chest, feeling the need to defend herself suddenly. Brenna, of all people, should understand her reservations. She'd kept Matt at arm's length for the longest time before giving in to her heart's yearning.

Brenna blew out a long, slow puff of air before addressing her friend. "Look, I know you spend a lot of time around horses instead of humans, but even you must see what the two of you have. Timing is just an excuse, because you're scared."

When Kate opened her mouth to disagree, Brenna put her hands up and shook her head. "No, this is one thing you just can't argue with. Remember, life is what happens when you're busy making other plans. Don't make the same mistakes I did. I tried to push Matt away because I was scared of what might happen if I let myself go. I made every excuse in the book, then told myself my reasons were justified. You're my friend, and I love you. Please don't let your fears steal your happiness."

"This isn't me being afraid. It's being realistic." Despite the look of concern on Brenna's face, Kate refused to change her mind. She'd almost changed it once by agreeing to go on that date with Jack and look what had happened as a result. Why couldn't her friend just accept things as they were, as they needed to be?

"My mom needs me right now, and I'm running out of time with her. I mean, how much longer do I have with her? *A week? A month? A year?* I don't know. It wouldn't be fair to my mother if I was distracted when I was with her, and it definitely wouldn't be fair to Jack to—"

Brenna raised an eyebrow, cutting Kate off at the quick. "So you admit you want more with Jack?"

She swallowed hard, ignoring Brenna's whispered comment.

"I get it," her friend continued. "You want to spend as much of your time with your mom as possible. No one is telling you that you shouldn't be doing that. But you need to live your life, too, Kate. You can't just put it on hold indefinitely. And I know your mom well enough to know she wouldn't want you to do that, either."

Kate kept her eyes focused on Hope as the young horse played in the distance. Howard stayed close by her as she ran and kicked and enjoyed her trip to the yard. A few times Kate held her breath, sure the little foal would tumble to the ground, but Hope had become surprisingly good on her feet and managed to keep all four under her.

Of course, she knew everything Brenna was saying was true. It had been true when Jack said it days ago as well. So why was it so hard for Kate to accept their words? Was she being a good and devoted daughter, or was she just using her mom's illness as an excuse because she didn't want to end up getting hurt?

Truthfully, she'd never even had a serious relationship— at least not to the point of falling in love. She'd never liked anyone that much, not until Jack.

With a sudden slam to her chest, she finally realized why she'd been holding back from a relationship with him. Yes, she wanted to be there for her mother, felt she owed it to her, but also she was afraid of becoming like her. Kate had never known her dad because he'd run out on them so early, but her mom had also never found love again after. All those years her mom had been on her own, with only Kate to love and support her. That sadness had left an indelible mark on her otherwise spirited mother.

Was that what was really stopping Kate from letting herself try with Jack?

Could it be that she was afraid to let love in because she worried what would happen when the happy feelings ran out? Because she would rather avoid love altogether than to risk failing at it?

She lifted her face to study the big house. Her heart walloped in her chest as she watched Jack exit through the front door, his eyes immediately connecting with her. She knew the moment he saw her because he stopped in his tracks, hesitating before he continued in her direction. She held her breath, unable to look away as he approached.

"Hi, Brenna. Kate." He hesitated only briefly before continuing. "Sorry to interrupt your visit, but I just got a call from one of the better facilities in Anchorage saying they might have a room available for your mother. They were wondering if I could bring you both in to check it out. They want a decision today, though. Otherwise they'll offer the vacancy to the next person on the list."

Kate glanced nervously toward her friend. She needed to act fast, especially if the opening was at the institution she suspected it might be. She'd put off her friend for so long, then hadn't even paid proper attention when they finally did get together. Now she planned to abandon her to visit the facility with Jack.

Some maid of honor she was turning out to be.

Brenna waved her off. "Don't worry about me. Go! This is too important to put off. We can talk about wedding stuff another time. Good luck."

"Thank you for understanding," Kate whispered to her friend as they hugged goodbye, all the while wondering if Brenna's wish for good luck had been about the facility or about something more. She'd have time to figure that out later, time to figure everything out—but right now, her mom needed her, which meant everything else needed to be put on hold.

She just hoped that by the time she had a chance to truly sit down and evaluate her life she'd still have options when it came to how to best live it.

And with whom.

CHAPTER 18

KATE SHIVERED AS SHE WALKED THROUGH THE PARKING LOT with Jack and her mother later that afternoon. Although the sun streamed down and birds were singing, none of the usual joy associated with such a fine day reached Kate. They'd capped off their tour of the rest home with ice cream provided by the staff. The facilities were remarkable, and the food was surprisingly good, but she wasn't sure how much her mother really understood about what their visit meant. At first her mom had been pleasant and polite, but as the tour wore on, she became distant and short with anyone who tried to address her directly.

Thankfully, Jack had patiently helped to keep everyone on task and ensure her mother was able to provide her input about the decision ahead. And because he'd worked with many patients from this facility in the past, he understood how everything worked and what kind of care she would receive.

If Kate had come on her own, she'd have easily been overwhelmed by all the new information and the far-reaching consequences of signing on the dotted line to assign her mother's care to the staff at the rest home. This made her incredibly grateful for Jack's help though she knew full well she didn't deserve it. She was so glad her mother hadn't suffered due to the poor way she'd chosen to end things with Jack.

"I'm glad you liked the room, Mom," she said before slipping into the back seat so that her mother could sit upfront. "That view from your window was gorgeous, and all the nurses and staff seemed absolutely wonderful. I can't believe how lucky we are to have landed a spot so quickly."

Her mother shrugged but otherwise ignored Kate's attempts to speak with her. She did not seem pleased about the forthcoming change.

Jack removed one hand from the steering wheel and reached over to squeeze her mother's hand. "I agree," he said. "This is the best place around, Nancy. And that ice cream was wow."

Her mother offered him a fleeting grin and nodded. While she seemed to blame Kate for this change in her care, she still loved being around Jack. Whether she remembered their connection or not was another matter entirely.

"We can get you moved in tomorrow, so just one last day stuck in the hospital. That's definitely something to celebrate." Jack let go of her hand and drummed on the steering wheel, trying his best to keep the mood light.

"Yeah, that's nice." Her mom's voice barely held any emotion at all.

Kate averted her eyes to the world outside the car window, trying not to let Jack or her mom see the pain in her eyes. All this time she'd worried about becoming a stranger to her mother, but now it felt like her mother was the one who'd become somebody else. Who was this frail, bored woman sitting in front of her? How could so much have changed in hardly any time at all?

"Mom, if you really don't like the room, we can keep looking," Kate said gently. Her voice choked slightly as she finally shifted her vision back toward the front of the car. "You just have to let me know."

"How much will it cost?" Her mom twisted in her seat and met Kate's eyes. Fear and worry shone clearly within them.

Kate startled at the sudden hostility in her voice. It seemed she could do nothing right anymore. "Don't worry about that, Mom. I'll take care of it."

"*No*. That's not how it's supposed to be," she snapped. "I'm your mother and I'm the one who is supposed to look after you. Stop treating me like I'm a child."

"You *have* looked after me. All my life, and I love you so much for it," Kate said, choking back a sob. "I hate what's happening to you and that I have no way to help you other than this. Please let me do this for you. Don't make it any harder than it already is."

Her stomach clenched in agony when she realized how sharp she'd just been with her mom. She hadn't meant to let her emotions take over her like that, and now her mom was staring at down her own hands as they fiddled with the seat-belt stretched across her lap.

"I'm sorry, Mom. I didn't mean to make you feel any worse." She looked to Jack in the rear-view mirror, hoping he would have some miraculous answer to make this all easier. He just smiled and mouthed the words telling her it would be okay.

Kate just couldn't bring herself to believe it.

"Mom?" she asked, placing a hesitant hand on her mother's arm.

She ripped it away as if she'd been burned, speaking to Kate in an irate tone she'd never used with her daughter before. "How dare you touch me!" she cried.

"I-I-I'm sorry," she stammered. Kate's eyes filled with

tears at the sudden outburst from her mom. "I was just trying to make sure you were okay."

"Who are you? Why do you care?" her mother shot back, caressing her arm and keeping it well out of Kate's reach even still.

Like a blow to the side of the head, Kate realized her mom truly didn't know and that she didn't have the strength to answer her.

Luckily, Jack came to the rescue. "Hey, Nancy. We'll have you back to your room in just a few minutes. Is there anything you want to pick up along the way?"

"No, thank you," her mother answered politely, her limbs letting go of some of the tension from earlier.

He continued to chatter with them both until they arrived at the hospital once more.

Kate stared ahead out the window into the dimly lit parking lot while Jack escorted her mother back inside. Her head rested on the back of the seat as she let the tears roll down her cheeks. She'd never felt so defeated in all her life. She hadn't even been able to get out of the car and had left Jack to see her mother back to her room. Maybe it was best her mom forgot her, because obviously Kate was a giant disappointment. At least she would forget the bad along with the good. Maybe that was something to be thankful for in the end.

She watched Jack approach the car, not even moving to

look at him when he opened the door and climbed back in. Immediately he reached for her hand, wrapping it in his own. "Kate, I'm sorry. I can't even imagine how you're feeling right now. But remember, it was an emotional day for her. By tomorrow, she might be completely different again. She loves you and hasn't forgotten who you are. Not for good, anyway."

Kate took a deep, shaky breath, not even sure if she could speak without completely breaking down. "I know that. But it's the first time she's forgotten me like that. Everything else has happened so fast. It's just a matter of time until she can't remember me at all. I don't know how to get through this." The words came out on a sob and before she knew what was happening, he had leaned over and wrapped her into his arms.

"It's going to be the hardest thing you'll ever have to do in your life, Kate. And it sucks. And it's not fair." He got out of the car and opened her door for her as well.

Immediately, she flew into his arms—not thinking, only feeling every horrible emotion she'd been trying so hard to hide from and feeling them all at once. She cried into his shoulder again, wishing her mother could be healthy again and that her own life would have turned out differently.

As Jack gently moved his hands through her hair and wiped the tears for her cheek, she wondered why she had fought so hard to keep away from him. It seemed that he was the only thing in her life that was right, and he was the one she'd been so quick to discard.

If she'd been a braver woman, she might have told him what was in her heart right then and there. Instead, Kate continued to sob and said nothing more as she fell apart in his arms.

CHAPTER 19

KATE SMILED OVER THE FENCE AS HOPE STOOD BESIDE THE old mare they'd recently put in the pen with her. Bonnie had lost a foal of her own a few months ago, and everyone was hopeful that Bonnie would adopt her and give her the companionship and guidance that could only come from another horse.

Blessedly, Bonnie was already starting to show signs of accepting Hope, occasionally moving to nuzzle the little filly.

"Well, Hope, it looks like you've found yourself a new mama. Treat her well." Kate mentally added "don't take her for granted." A familiar ache in her chest threatened to overtake Kate.

Of course, she was glad that Hope had someone new to look after her. But on the other hand, she felt a sense of loss knowing that this was the start of saying goodbye for good.

Hope was starting to nibble at some hay and grain now but would still require the milk supplement for a couple more months. After that, she would be able to survive without any added intervention.

"It's amazing to see her now," Jack said as he suddenly popped up next to Kate. "Hard to believe just a couple weeks ago she didn't even look like she'd survive the night."

"I didn't hear you coming," Kate said in a breathy whisper to explain the fact that she'd jumped upon his arrival. She turned suddenly to face him and noticed he had two horses out beside him. "Now I feel worse. How'd I miss you plus two horses? And why do you have Buddy?"

Jack shrugged noncommittally, keeping his face neutral as he spoke. "I thought we could go for a ride. It's beautiful out today and it would be shame to waste this chance."

She shook her head. "I can't. I've got work to do around the barn."

"Howard said they can manage fine for a couple hours. C'mon. When's the last time you went for a ride just for the fun of it?"

Jack reached out and took her hand. "Stop overthinking. Buddy is waiting for you." He pulled her over to Buddy's side, and the gentle gelding turned his head to sniff at her hair.

"It *has* been a while, but—"

Buddy stomped impatiently.

"Sheesh, you too, Buddy?" She chuckled. How had Jack managed to get the horses on his side to help lure her away from work?

Jack's hands wrapped around her waist as he helped her climb up into the saddle. Normally she'd have scoffed at anyone trying to help her with something she'd already done a million times on her own, but today she let herself enjoy the feeling of getting some help from another person without even needing to ask.

"Okay, what now?" Kate asked as Jack threw himself onto his own horse's back, then adjusted himself in the saddle.

"Race you to the top of that hill." He pointed to the far end of the path that led from the stables and looked over the valley below. A large tree stood sentinel at the top. Liz and Dorian had actually placed a bench beneath it for riders to use as a rest point while enjoying the view of the countryside.

"To that big tree," he finished with a smirk.

Without waiting for him to even say go, Kate spurred Buddy into action.

"Hey! Cheater!" she heard him cry out as she flew past.

There was something incredibly soothing about riding on the back of a horse as it galloped. With the rhythmic pounding of hooves on the ground, the crisp spring wind whipping around her face, something primal reached her deep into her soul. Why hadn't she been letting these beautiful creatures help to heal her all along?

She leaned forward in the saddle, smiling unrestrained in a moment of pure bliss. This was something she'd missed dearly, though she could have accessed it all this time.

As they crested the hill, Kate reined Buddy in and wheeled him around to watch Jack struggling to catch up. His dark hair moved in the wind as he raced up the field behind them. The way he sat high in the center saddle proved he had most definitely grown up around horses.

"I could've won that," he said, grinning as he pulled up next to her and Buddy. The horse's sides heaved with the exertion of the run, matching Kate's own labored breathing.

"No, you couldn't have. Buddy is the fastest horse here. I might've neglected to mention that." She laughed as he dropped his head in defeat.

"Doomed from the start," he lamented with a sad chuckle. He threw his leg over the back of his horse and dropped to the ground before leading his horse over to the grassy spot beside the bench on the hill. The horse immediately put his head down to graze.

Kate dismounted and guided Buddy to join in the mid-ride snack, then sunk down onto the bench. As she looked down onto the valley, she could see that breakup would soon be over and a full-fledged spring would be upon them. Packs of snow and mud were quickly being replaced with vegetation and new life blooming below. There were signs of new buds all over the trees, and the faded colors closer to the earth had begun the transformation into vibrant, lively shades of green.

She leaned her head back and breathed in deeply. "No matter how many times I've lived through it, the coming of spring always feels like a wonderful gift. Everything comes back to life after so long in hiding. It's just so… beautiful."

In the tree above them the birds sang their hearts out, finally able to enjoy the warmer weather after living through the coldest months.

"Almost as beautiful as you." Jack sat down beside her and put his arm around her shoulder, pulling her in close.

Her immediate reaction was to tense up and pull away, but she fought that instinct and let her body relax into his. If the earth could reawaken after such a long sleep, well, then maybe Kate could come back to life, too.

"I brought you here because we need to talk," Jack explained, his breath warm against her forehead as he spoke. "That's why I devised this cunning plan to bring you just far enough away that you could be yourself. Plus, it'll be harder for you to run away from me out here."

She rolled her eyes in mock irritation. "As if I'd run away from you."

He sat quietly for a moment. "Kate, you've been running

from me for weeks," he said quietly, his voice little more than a whisper.

She sat up, ready to debate, but Jack held up a hand to ward her off.

"No, Kate. Please, just listen."

She leaned into him once more. She could feel his chest rumbling beneath her shoulder as he spoke.

"I hate what you're going through and that you feel like you need to do this alone. And I hate the fact that Alzheimer's disease can rob so much from people. It's hard feeling so helpless and watching you suffer through this, Kate. I've seen it with other people and it's never easy, but with you, it feels like my heart is being ripped from my chest every time I see the pain in your eyes. I know you're going to be angry with me, but I don't know any other way to get through to you. I'm going to put it bluntly, not to be mean, but in the hopes that it will finally help."

Kate felt like she was on the edge of a cliff about to hurtle over the edge. Whatever Jack had to say would surely be something she'd already thought hundreds of times in her own mind.

But when he licked his lips and fixed his eyes on her, his voice barely came out above whisper and he surprised her with what he said next. "The thing I hate the most about all of this, is watching you die with your mom."

CHAPTER 20

KATE JUMPED TO HER FEET AND STARED AT JACK IN SHOCK. "How can you say that?"

"Because it's the truth," he replied with a weary sigh. "I'm sorry, but I've stood back watching you die a bit every day and I would give anything—I'd give *everything*—to take this disease away so you can have your mom. But unfortunately that's not something I can do, as much as I wish I could. Your mother is dying and it's a terrible, awful thing... but that doesn't mean your light has to go out, too."

"Just go, then," she shouted. Her voice shook with anger. "I'm not forcing you to be around me or my mom."

Jack stood and tried to put a hand on her shoulder, but she stepped away, still unwilling to look at him.

"You're the one who keeps coming back," she continued, tears stinging at her eyes. "I've told you I can't be who you need me to be right now. My mom needs me more than you do, and I'm all she has left. I can't just go on being happy while she's out there *dying.*"

Dying. It hurt so much to say that word, but it was also the truth.

"Yes, you've told me over and over how you need to focus on your mom. But can't you see that you can still be there for your mom while living your own life, too? I know you think you're some kind of long-suffering paragon, but that's not what's happening here. No. You're being selfish, because you're using your mom's illness to keep the walls up around you so no one can get in."

Kate turned to glare at him, her eyes narrowing with full-blown rage. "How dare you!" she shouted through tears.

"You can get as angry with me as you want. I've danced around your feelings for a long time, but it's not helping anyone, least of all you. Hate me forever if you want, but this was something you needed to hear."

She shook with anger, sorrow, so many more emotions she couldn't even begin to understand. Rather than addressing Jack's claims, she bit the inside of her cheek to distract herself. But nothing could compare to the pain emanating from her heart.

Jack's voice softened, but still he kept his distance. "You're right, I do keep coming back. Know why? It's because I love you, Kate. I love you, and I want to help, but

147

no matter how hard I try, you won't let me. I can't keep standing here watching you do this to yourself anymore. I'm sorry if I've hurt you, and maybe someday you can forgive me. But I love you too much to just let you fade away like this without at least trying to make a difference."

She struggled to breathe against the pain in her chest. He'd said he loved her. No one besides her mother had ever said those words to her—and the way things were going, she'd never hear those words from her mom again. Now she only had Jack...

That is, if she was willing to accept his love without any more questions or hesitations.

She didn't know what to say, so they stood in silence listening to the birds singing and the horse's hooves stomping on the ground behind them.

Finally, when it became clear that neither had anything more to say, Jack reached into his pocket, pulled out an envelope, and handed it to her. "One of the therapy exercises I did with your mother was to have her write letters to the people who mattered most in her life. She only wrote one. To you. She was supposed to have this conversation with you in person, but we could never get you into a shared session. Maybe she just wasn't ready to have that talk face-to-face, I don't know. And I don't know what she wrote in this letter or even that I should be giving it to you now, but

I'm willing to take the chance. If my words won't make a difference, then perhaps hers will."

He turned and hopped back onto his horse. "Goodbye, Kate. If you ever need me, you know where I am." He wheeled his horse around again began a leisurely pace back to the ranch house.

Kate slumped back onto the bench, holding the envelope tightly between her fingers as she watched Jack ride out of her life. She'd thought an already broken heart couldn't keep hurting, but she'd been so wrong. And now her inability to be brave had caused Jack's heart to break as well.

With a deep, centering breath, she tore into the envelope, unwilling to wait even another second to read its contents. While she was afraid of what she would find within, she had to know. Perhaps it was the only thing that could save her now that she'd chased Jack away and refused to take the steps needed to save herself.

Glancing down, she saw her mother's familiar handwriting looked a bit more jagged and rough than it had been years ago, but still she recognized it immediately. Kate took another deep breath, steadying her hands, and did her best to make out the words through tear-filled eyes.

My dearest Kate,

By the time you read this, my disease will most likely have ravaged my body to the point where I'm not the same person you have always known. I'm so sorry that you've been put through this. If there was any way I could have taken away the pain I know you're going through, I would.

But life sometimes deals us cards we aren't sure how to play. Unfortunately, this is a hand I can't win, no matter how much I want to.

We've been through so much together, and I worry about what will happen to you when I'm gone. You deserve happiness, Kate. You deserve the love of a man who will make you his world, and you deserve the chance to have a family of your own.

I would never trade what we had for anything because I've always loved how it was—you and me against the world. Still, that's me. I know it would have been nice for you to have a family—more than just me. If I could have found someone to trust, I could have given you that. Instead, I let my fear over getting hurt again stand in the way of giving you everything you needed then.

Everything you need still.

Don't let the same thing happen to you. Don't ever give up on yourself.

Live.

And love.

Find someone who brings you joy and who you can count on to always be there for you. I don't want to think of you spending the rest of your life alone.

You deserve so much more from your life.

Please, for me, go out and live. Honor me and my memory by giving yourself the chance at happiness.

Always remember that I love you and I'm so proud of the woman you've become. Even when it happens that I'm no longer able to remember you, know that your memory is in my heart. And I will always be in yours.

Be happy, Kate.

Love always,

Mom

WHEN KATE LIFTED her eyes again, she could just barely make out the faint outline of Jack dismounting and leading his horse through the gate of the stables in the distance. Her breath caught when she thought he turned to look back up toward her, but then she realized he was just talking to Howard. He handed the reins over to the older cowboy and made his way around the stables and out of sight.

She looked down at her trembling hands that gripped her mother's letter so tight. Her mom wanted her to be happy just like everyone had been telling her this whole time. She'd been so afraid of abandoning her mom she didn't even realize that she was making things worse by going against what she wanted for Kate.

Jack had been right.

She was the problem. No one else.

She thought back to the time Jack had told her she didn't have to choose, that he wasn't making her do that. He'd simply been asking for the chance to be a part of her life going forward. And now he'd even confessed that he loved her, but she'd ignored his brave, heartfelt words.

Because she was still so scared.

Maybe she would always be scared.

And maybe—just maybe—she had to do it anyway.

She'd already lost her mom to the disease.

And now she prayed that she hadn't also lost Jack to her own foolish fears.

CHAPTER 21

THE TRANSFORMATION TO SPRING WAS COMPLETE, BRINGING with it the first weddings of the season. In the week that had followed her confrontation with Jack on the high hill she'd managed to move her mother to assisted living, put in her two weeks' notice at the ranch, and attend to her final, last-minute maid of honor duties for Brenna.

Spring was about new beginnings, and Kate was almost upon a new chapter of her own life now, too. She came upon it wiser, battle-worn, and more than ready to make a change.

Her closest friend Brenna was undergoing a new trans-formation as well, but unlike Kate, she was emerging as the most beautiful of butterflies. Kate waited at the front of the decorated pole barn, watching Brenna walk down the aisle.

Her groom smiled from ear to ear, a glazed look of puppy love in his eyes.

When Brenna's mom offered her daughter's hand to Matt, a lump formed in Kate's throat. Brenna's father had died, leaving it up to her mother to give her away today. If Kate ever got the chance to walk down the aisle, she would need to do it on her own. There would be no one left to give her away.

Brenna and Matt joined hands before the minister, each sobbing silent tears of joy.

Kate scanned the crowd until she found Jack. He looked so handsome in his light blue shirt and khaki pants, his hair just as purposefully disheveled as always. He didn't notice Kate. Instead, his eyes were fixed on the happy couple as they listened to the sermon with rapt attention. Could Kate have ended up here with him if only she'd been brave?

That possibility didn't bear thinking about.

Today was Brenna's day.

And Kate was so happy for her friend. Brenna deserved this. Matt did, too.

As they said their vows, Kate's far-off smile never left her face. She could feel the pure love between the two of them, and it made her truly happy to witness. Theirs was the kind of love you only saw in movies or read about in books, and their self-written vows proved it.

The ceremony ended quickly—such a short bit of time for such a life-altering event.

A cheer erupted through the crowd as Matt took Brenna in his arms and gave her a kiss that lasted almost as long as the rest of the ceremony. When Matt and Brenna broke apart, Kate and the rest of the bridal party dug into the coolers they'd hidden behind the altar and unleashed a torrent of snowballs on the guests.

Kate giggled as Jack took one straight in the forehead. When he laughed, too, her heart felt weightless within her chest. Maybe she still had time. Perhaps she could emerge a butterfly, too.

Since breakup was complete, the guests had no recourse as the bridesmaids and groomsmen pelted them with their off-season ammo. It didn't take long to run out of snowballs, though. They marched down the aisle to cheers and jeers and shouts of congratulations. As Kate passed Jack, she felt the heat of his gaze press into her.

As much as she wanted to stop and throw her arms around him and tell him everything in her heart, she would never upstage her friend's big day. And what would she even tell him, anyway?

She'd spent the past several nights tossing and turning as she tried to figure everything out. After reading her mom's letter, she'd realized she was going to have to do something or she would lose her chance with

Jack forever. But simply saying sorry didn't seem like enough, either. How could she possibly make him understand something she didn't quite understand yet for herself?

So instead she'd done nothing, not yet. Oh, how she hoped the wedding celebration today would give her the strength to finally reveal what was in her heart—what had been there all along.

They finished their return march down the aisle and started the receiving line. Kate was the first to throw her arms around her friend and offer her sincere congratulations. "I'm so happy for you, Brenna. You look so beautiful, today. I'm so glad you asked me to be a part of this."

Brenna clutched her tightly. "Thank you, Kate. I'm glad you've been with me leading up to this. You've been like another sister."

They smiled widely at each other. Having a friend as dear to her as Brenna had become meant the world to Kate. She couldn't imagine her life without her. And even though she'd always thought it was just her and her mom over the years, Kate was now learning to trust other people enough to let them be a part of that life, too.

"Hey, remember me? I'm the one who's supposed to be standing here in my bride's arms today," Matt interrupted, grinning as he put his arm around Brenna's shoulders. Matt was a good man, and she was so glad Brenna had found him.

THE HAPPIEST PLACE

She'd known him for a long time now and had seen the kindness that pulsed with every beat of his heart.

"Congratulations, Matt," she said, hugging him, too. "You got a good one."

Even as the words came from her mouth, she could hear her mother's voice saying a version of the same thing to her.

Matt flushed, his entire face turning red to match his hair. "I could say the same to you," he said with a wry grin. "I'm pretty sure there's a man over there who hasn't taken his eyes off you since we got here."

Of course, Matt knew Jack well from being at the ranch. Kate also suspected Brenna had revealed Kate's almost relationship to him at some point.

When the receiving line petered out, Brenna and Matt moved to the makeshift dance floor that was most often used in the barn for events and seasonal dances at the ranch. Jack's brother, Marty, had volunteered as DJ and knew the exact right moment to start the music the couple had selected for their first dance.

Even though Kate knew that Brenna had chosen Lonestar's *Amazed* as their special song, hearing it now still caused her heart to clench for what she'd willingly abandoned. She watched the newlyweds move around the dance floor, lost in each other's eyes, and imagined it was her out there.

Her and Jack.

"C'mon now, everybody," Marty's voice came over the

2

speakers. "Brenna and Matt would like their friends and family to join them up here."

Kate knew she was supposed to be a part of this, but she just couldn't bring herself to stand by and watch as all the happy couples formed around her. She spun on her heel in a desperate attempt to escape for some fresh air, but bumped straight into someone's chest before she could even make it off the dance floor.

"Oh, sorry," she mumbled.

"Don't be," Jack said, offering his hand as an invitation.

She lifted her eyes to his, searching for the answers she'd been too afraid to give all this time. "Jack, I…"

"Let's just dance," he said, swaying with her right where they stood. The song sounded like it was a million miles away now, and all Kate could hear was the beating of his heart as she placed her head on his chest.

This. This was what she wanted. Not just now, but forever.

When the song ended, she grabbed his hand and pulled him outside among the dim, flickering lights that had been set up around the yard like fairies in the night. She dragged him toward the stables, feeling better knowing Hope was nearby. That sweet little horse had overcome much greater hardships than Kate had ever faced and was flourishing now. She'd given everyone at the ranch hope that better things were ahead.

Kate took a deep breath, swallowed down all her fears, and gripped Jack's hands for extra strength—and for a reminder of just how much she could still lose.

She started by saying the thing that needed to be said the most, "I'm sorry. I'm sorry for pushing you away and not letting myself believe what I was feeling. You've done so much for me and never asked for anything in return except for a chance at us. I know I haven't been fair, and I don't blame you if you've already given up on me. The truth is, being with me right now *won't* be easy. I'm going through something that is so difficult, some days I don't even know if I want to get out of bed. But having you by my side through it all would mean everything to me. It would give me a reason to try harder, to be better. And it would give me a chance to be happy."

She knew her words were spilling out of her mouth so quickly he probably couldn't even keep up, but now that the floodgates had opened, she needed to keep the flow of her confession moving.

He remained silent, waiting for her to say more.

She still hadn't said the most important thing of all.

She reached a hesitant hand toward his face, stroking the smooth skin of his freshly shaven cheek. She studied him carefully as she said, "You said you love me. And I love you, too, Jack. I love you so, so much. And if you'll give me another chance, I want you by my side through it all."

He smiled and closed one hand over hers, bringing the other up to touch her face. "Kate, no matter what you might have thought, there's no way I was ever going to leave your side."

His lips found hers and she finally knew how right her mother had been.

Not just about Jack, but about everything.

Finally, this was her chance to be happy.

EPILOGUE

K<small>ATE</small> <small>LAUGHED AS SHE WATCHED</small> H<small>OPE PRANCE GIANT</small>, frenetic circles around her new adoptive mother, Bonnie. Despite being a much older horse, Bonnie enjoyed the young foal's company and also played and ran with her on occasion —and Hope was absolutely smitten with her.

Buddy lifted his head from across the yard to see what the fuss was about but quickly decided the energetic foal wasn't anything for him to get excited about and returned his full attention to grazing. Finally, Hope had been accepted as part of the group, and Bonnie made sure none of the others gave her any trouble.

Kate leaned back against the tree and closed her eyes as she listened to the horses whinny and neigh. The warm August sun beat down on her cheeks as she tipped her face toward the sky. It was Kate's birthday and another beautiful

Saturday on the ranch. Her friends and coworkers had all decided it was the perfect day for a picnic celebration. Now they were just waiting for the final member of their party to arrive before digging in.

Jack, of all people, was the one holding things up today.

Marty and the rest of his family members were the first to arrive, but Liz had immediately scooped them up for a grand tour of the ranch. Kate enjoyed waiting in the company of the horses, smiling to herself as she realized that all the people she had met and cared about over the past few months had all come together to celebrate her birthday.

Well, almost everyone. The staff at her mother's care facility thought it would be a bad idea to take her away from the rest home, but Kate planned to stop by that evening for a private celebration with just her and her mom.

As hard as everything still was, it got a little easier each day—or at least Kate became better equipped to deal with it. It would never be easy witnessing the effects of her mother's disease, but she'd finally come to accept what she could and couldn't change.

She couldn't make her mom magically better.

But she could make the most of the time they had left.

She could let others in and lean on them in times of need.

She could be happy. She wanted to be happy not just for herself, but for her mom, too.

In the weeks since Brenna and Matt's wedding, her mom's health had continued to decline. She still had good days, though—and on those days, Kate was sure her mom could still remember the most important things. She stored these special moments in her heart to help her get through the bad ones, to keep moving forward with her new life while honoring the past they'd shared together.

At last the silhouette of Jack appeared on the path leading in from the big house. Kate hadn't seen him since yesterday and couldn't wait to feel his arms around her again.

As he drew closer, she noticed that he wasn't alone, but the sun in her eyes made it hard for her to see who accompanied him. *Who is that?*

Kate's breath caught in her throat when she realized who he'd brought to her party. "Mom!" she cried.

She hadn't seen her mother outside of a facility since the night she'd been taken from the ranch in the ambulance all those months ago. Kate wanted to run to her, but Brenna stopped her.

"Wait here," her friend urged with a knowing smile.

"But it's my mom," Kate said, crying unabashedly happy tears. "I can't believe she's here."

Brenna placed a hand on Kate's shoulder to keep her from running off. "Let him bring your mom to you. Just wait right here."

163

Kate glanced around her, confused as she watched Jack's parents come out of the barn with Liz. Her coworkers all appeared then, too. Everyone held collapsible chairs, and everyone looked so, so happy.

Marty came over and stood beside Brenna with a huge grin on his face. He handed her a bouquet of wildflowers from the ranch and said, "You look beautiful today, Kate."

Marty was the sweetest and kindest person she'd ever met, and she knew without a doubt he was someone who would always be in her corner—but was he in on some kind of conspiracy with the others? She couldn't believe that they'd all managed to keep this surprise from her, and she still had no idea what was coming next.

Jack made his way over slowly with her mom and finally stopped in front of Kate. His smile was the widest of them all.

"Mom, it's so good to see you." Kate mouthed a quick thank you to him, pulling her mom into her arms for a hug and hoping today was one of her good days. It meant so much to have her here.

"Thank you, dear," her mother said with a kindly but otherwise blank expression.

Jack grabbed Kate's hand and gave it a kiss. "I have a confession to make. Your mom isn't here just for your birthday. None of us are."

Jack looked at her sheepishly as he squeezed her hand and widened his eyes with boyish mirth.

Kate took in the smiling crowd around them and turned back to Jack. "What do you mean?"

"What I mean," he said, dropping to one knee in the grass. "Is that I love you more than anything, and I want you to be my wife. *Today*," he added with another playful flash in his eyes.

Her mouth hung open as she slowly looked over and realized why Marty and Brenna were still standing beside her grinning like fools.

"Your mom is here today to give you away. That is, if you'll have me." He spoke the last part quietly enough that only she could here.

Kate still stood staring at him in shock. Her mom looked happy, but Kate couldn't be sure how much she actually understood. Heck, she was having a hard time understanding herself.

"Kate?" Jack remained crouched down as he waited for an answer. Everyone around them waited, too. Even Hope ventured over to the nearest stretch of fence and gave a loud whinny to let Kate know she was there and waiting, too.

What was she waiting for?

Jack had offered her the perfect gift. Not just this day. Not just her mother's presence, but the most precious gift of all—his heart.

Finally, she nodded, unable to say anything for fear it wouldn't be perfect enough to match this moment.

Jack popped back to his feet and gave a giant whoop, then took her mother's arm gently and looped it through Kate's. He leaned down and kissed her quickly before heading up to the tree with Marty at his side. She had no idea when the minister had joined them, but there he was, ready to perform the ceremony that would change Kate's life once and for all.

Just a few short months ago, Kate had served as Brenna's maid of honor, and now her friend was able to return the favor today.

Brenna gave her a quick hug. "Are you ready?"

Kate nodded, feeling like everything around her was moving in blessedly slow motion. To be honest, she never wanted this moment to end. But then Brenna strolled up the short path to the tree in true bridal procession, and everyone rose from their chairs in anticipation of Kate's grand walk down this beautiful aisle of nature.

She looked over at her mom, who reached up to put a hand on her daughter's cheek. "You're a very beautiful girl."

Kate fought against the lump that formed in her throat upon realizing her mother most likely didn't know her today. But in the grand scheme of things, that didn't matter. She was here beside Kate on the most important day of all her life—and her birthday, too. It was more than she could have possibly hoped for.

Together, they march toward Jack. Even though this turn of events had come on suddenly, Kate was so ready to be his wife. When they reached her groom waiting by the tree, Kate leaned forward and kissed her mother's cheek. "I love you, Mom," she whispered.

Her mother smiled proudly, tears had even begun to form at the corners of her eyes. And then she said the most amazing thing. "I love you, Kate. Be happy."

Kate was so astonished, she choked back a sob. Her mother was here for her in every sense of the word. She knew her, she knew what they were doing, and she had given her blessing.

She accepted a kiss from her mom before turning to Jack at their makeshift altar with more love than she ever though she could possibly feel for anyone besides her mother.

But there Jack was. And here Kate was.

They may have gone through hell to get here, but now, as her new husband clasped her hands in his and declared his undying and eternal love, Kate knew they had found their own small piece of heaven.

Are you ready to read Sofia's story? She's on a noble mission to rescue hurt and neglected dogs...

too bad it requires breaking the law to complete it.

CLICK HERE to get your copy of *The Darkest Hour,* so that you can keep reading this series today!

And make sure you're on Melissa's list so that you hear about all her new releases, special giveaways, and other sweet bonuses.

You can do that here: MelStorm.com/gift

WHAT'S NEXT?

Sofia Stepanov believes in right and wrong, but she doesn't necessarily believe in following the rules. When she finds a wolf hybrid being illegally kept and abused by its captors, she vows to come back and free him herself.

Soon the exhilaration of one successful mission leads to many more, leading Sofia to set her sights on the most ambitious rescue yet. It also leads her straight into the path of a handsome police officer who has been tasked with bringing Anchorage's serial dognapper to justice.

Will Sofia complete her vigilante rescue without a hitch, or will Hunter catch her before she can?

Join Sophia and Liz with their rehabilitated sled dogs in this unforgettable tale of resourcefulness, repercussions, and finding where you belong. Start reading THE DARKEST HOUR today!

The Darkest Hour is now available.

CLICK HERE to get your copy so that you can keep reading this series today!

SNEAK PEEK OF THE DARKEST HOUR

Sofia Stepanov's journey toward happily ever after started the way so many do—with a beautiful, tortured pair of eyes staring straight into her soul.

She gulped before taking a closer look. These eyes didn't belong to a charming prince, but rather a mottled gray dog chained to a stake in somebody's front yard.

Help me, those striking amber orbs begged, but Sofia rolled past the stop sign and continued toward her destination. It's not that she was heartless, though sometimes her friends teased that stodgy Sofia kept her heart locked up tight in a tiny box hidden deep within her chest.

She wanted to help the poor, neglected mutt, but what could she do? She was already late for work. She didn't have a lick of experience owning a pet, and stealing was just a touch against the law.

Regardless, Sofia thought about that poor, scraggly creature the whole day, ultimately making a deal with herself. *If I drive past there tonight and he's still out there, then I'll break him free.*

And, sure enough, the dog she'd taken to calling "Wolfie" in her mind remained chained in place when she drove back through the dilapidated Mountain View neighborhood more than eight hours later.

She'd "borrowed" a leash from the mall's pet store on her way home from work, reasoning that she didn't have to pay if it was only meant to be a loan. Besides, she was doing the Lord's work, protecting his creatures and all that.

Yeah, it definitely would have been far worse to do nothing. The universe *wanted* her to free this poor sap of a dog, and so she would.

She drove by the yard a few times just to make sure that no one was home, then parked down the block and began her rescue mission.

Wolfie let out a low whine as she approached. He kept his head and body on the ground, but slowly, hopefully, began to thump his tail in the dirt beneath him.

No bared teeth—a good sign if ever there was one.

Sofia had never kept a pet growing up, then hadn't wanted the added responsibility once she'd finally struck out on her own. Even so, she'd always had a way with animals, especially the downtrodden ones. They seemed to somehow sense a kindred spirit in her which, she had to admit, *was* accurate.

Nobody had ever chained Sofia to a stake, but they'd done plenty of awful things to her growing up. Gossip, rumors, pranks, all the usual mean girl fodder had all been directed squarely at Sofia.

In seventh grade, she'd gone through an adolescent revolution and finally found out exactly who she was meant to be, which unfortunately also meant finding herself as the official Bartlett High outcast. Previously a blonde, pink-cheeked clone of her mother, Sofia had dyed her hair black and never looked back. She'd begun avoiding the sun as if she really were a vampire, like one of the less imaginative rumors about her had claimed.

And now here she was, creeping around at night, getting ready to steal somebody's dog.

Not steal—*rescue*.

She had to remind herself of that over and over again until she was sure she believed it. Sofia was the good guy here. Had always been.

Reaching into her bag, she wrapped her fingers around the food court hotdog she'd picked up for just this purpose.

Wolfie's whining intensified when he saw the snack.

"You want this, boy? Yeah?" Sofia tiptoed up to the dog

and handed him the hotdog while she switched the chain for the leash.

Quick, quick. There. Atta boy.

Checking that the clasp was secure, she removed a second hotdog from her bag and flashed it before the dog. "We have to hurry, okay? Just follow me, and I'll give you another one of these. Got it?"

Wolfie barked, his tail swinging at a frenzied pace.

"Shhhh," Sofia warned, slowly letting herself back out through the gate with Wolfie in tow. "Let's go."

If anyone saw the dognapping in action, they did nothing to stop it. It was almost too easy. Sofia kept waiting for an angry, gun-waving homeowner or the whir of sirens, but nothing happened. It felt like mere seconds. One moment, she was just passing by, and the next she'd somehow become a dog owner.

Did easy mean right? Well, she guessed time would tell on that one.

So now what?

What happens next?
Don't wait to find out...

Read the next two chapters right now in Melissa Storm's free book app.

Or head to my website to purchase your copy so that you can keep reading this sweet, heartwarming series today!

Special Collections & Boxed Sets

From light-hearted comedies to stories about finding hope in the darkest of times, these special boxed editions offer a great way to catch up or to fall in love with Melissa Storm's books for the first time.

Alaskan Hearts: Books 1-3

Alaskan Hearts: Books 4-6

The Church Dogs of Charleston: Books 1-3

The First Street Church Romances: Books 1-3

The Sweet Promise Press Collection

The Alaska Sunrise Romances: Books 1-3

The Alaska Sunrise Romances: Books 4-6

The Alaska Sunrise Romances: Books 7-9

The Sunday Potluck Club

Because nothing satisfies like friendship...

Home Sweet Home

The Sunday Potluck Club

Wednesday Walks and Wags

The Church Dogs of Charleston

A very special litter of Chihuahua puppies born on Christmas day is adopted by the local church and immediately set to work as tiny therapy dogs.

The Long Walk Home

The Broken Road to You

The Winding Path to Love

Alaskan Hearts: Sled Dogs

Get ready to fall in love with a special pack of working and retired sled dogs, each of whom change their new owners' lives for the better.

The Loneliest Cottage

The Brightest Light

The Truest Home

The Darkest Hour

Alaskan Hearts: Memory Ranch

This sprawling ranch located just outside Anchorage helps its patients regain their lives, love, and futures.

The Sweetest Memory

The Strongest Love

The Happiest Place

The First Street Church Romances

Sweet and wholesome small town love stories with the community church at their center make for the perfect feel-good reads!

Love's Prayer

Love's Promise

Love's Prophet

Love's Vow

Love's Trial

Sweet Promise Press

What's our Sweet Promise? It's to deliver the heartwarming, entertaining, clean, and wholesome reads you love with every single book.

Saving Sarah

Flirting with the Fashionista

Stand-Alone Novels and Novellas

Whether climbing ladders in the corporate world or taking care of things at home, every woman has a story to tell.

A Mother's Love

A Colorful Life

Love & War

Do you know that Melissa also writes humorous Cozy Mysteries as Molly Fitz? Click below to check them out: **www.MollyMysteries.com**

MEET THE AUTHOR

Melissa Storm is a New York Times and multiple USA Today bestselling author of Women's Fiction and Inspirational Romance.

Despite an intense, lifelong desire to tell stories for a living, Melissa was "too pragmatic" to choose English as a major in college. Instead, she obtained her master's degree in Sociology & Survey Methodology—then went straight back to slinging words a year after graduation anyway.

She loves books so much, in fact, that she married fellow author Falcon Storm. Between the two of them, there are always plenty of imaginative, awe-inspiring stories to share. Melissa and Falcon also run a number of book-related businesses together, including LitRing, Sweet Promise Press, Novel Publicity, and Your Author Engine.

When she's not reading, writing, or child-rearing, Melissa spends time relaxing at her home in the Michigan woods, where she is kept company by a seemingly unending quantity of dogs and two very demanding Maine Coon rescues. She also writes under the names of Molly Fitz and Mila Riggs.

CONNECT WITH MELISSA

You can download my free app here:
melstorm.com/app

Or sign up for my newsletter and receive an exclusive free story, *Angels in Our Lives*, along with new release alerts, themed giveaways, and uplifting messages from Melissa!
melstorm.com/gift

Or maybe you'd like to chat with other animal-loving readers as well as to learn about new books and giveaways as soon as they happen! Come join Melissa's VIP reader group on Facebook.
melstorm.com/group

Made in the USA
Monee, IL
03 April 2021

64762446R00105